Mis'

Dragonfire

Misha Herwin

authorHOUSE®

AuthorHouse™ UK Ltd.
500 Avebury Boulevard
Central Milton Keynes, MK9 2BE
www.authorhouse.co.uk
Phone: 08001974150

First published by AuthorHouse 1/7/2008

ISBN: 978-1-4343-4419-9 (sc)

Printed in the United States of America
Bloomington, Indiana

This book is printed on acid-free paper.

ACKNOWLEDGEMENTS

There are lots of people who have helped to make Dragonfire, but I would like to say a special thank you to all my family, especially my mum and uncle, who read the first draft and liked it; my sister for her comments and my nephews Sebastian and Peter for theirs.

The members of Room in the Roof, for their unfailing support and helpful critiques. Don't know what I'd have done without you guys.

Emma and David Rowland who read the manuscript and gave their approval

And of course their uncle Guy, for everything.

Alishea, Alex, Lizzie, Jeorgia, Emily, Chelsea, Rhiannon, Sarah, Ailsa, Sam, Robert, Jonathan, Adam and Matthew, my writing group at St. Edwards, who brainstormed the fantastic title.

My friends for their belief in me.

And Mike, who kept me sane, even when I was driving him crazy.

For Posy David and Lucy.

All leading characters in this book are based on real people. With their permission, of course.

CHAPTER ONE

"There were dragons in the sky, the night the firework factory blew up," Gran said. Courtleigh shuffled uncomfortably his seat. He looked up at the clock on the wall and wondered how much longer he would have to wait. "It was a sign. I know it was. A sign of evil and change, but one good thing came out of it," Gran smiled and patted his knee. "It brought me you."

Courtleigh looked at his little Gran with her black skin as wrinkled as a walnut, her bright coloured dress and the gold tooth, that flashed when she grinned, and wondered why she was telling him all this. He knew the story of how the ground had opened up after the explosion and the block of flats, where he lived with his mum, had been swallowed up, never to be seen again. Gran blamed the dragons fighting. She said it was terrible battle and he was lucky to have survived.

"I found you in the morning," she continued. "You came running to me out of the smoke and dust. You and this baby were the only two left alive. Your Mamma was gone and your Daddy was on his travels, so it was up to me to bring you up."

"I know," Courtleigh muttered. His stomach was churning and his mouth was dry.

"I did my best," Gran said softly. "Whatever happens, I want you to remember that."

"Courtleigh Jones," the usher stood in the doorway. "They are ready for you now." His footsteps echoed on the marble floor, as he led the way into the gloomy courtroom.

Mrs Whiteside, the magistrate, glared at the boy in front of her. Her fat, white face looked as if it had been carved out of lard. There was a long black hair growing out of the mole on her chin and a faint moustache over her top lip. She hated teenagers, especially jumped up lads who swaggered around thinking they knew everything.

"If I had my way, Courtleigh Jones, I would have you locked up and the key thrown away," she said.

"Yes Mam," he muttered. He thrust his hands in his pockets and stared at the floor.

Here she goes again, he thought, as Mrs Whiteside banged her fist on the desk and leaned towards him.

"Look at me Courtleigh," she snarled.

She looks like a pig, he thought. *In a minute she'll start snorting and grunting and she'll get down on all fours and run out of the court and I can go home with Gran.* He bit the inside of his mouth, but it was too late, the grin spread over his face and Mrs Whiteside was turning purple with fury.

"You find this funny, do you?" she screamed. "Let me tell you this. I have done everything possible to get you back onto the straight and narrow. It's typical of boys your age that nothing I do seems to make any difference. I have tried fines; I have tried putting you on probation and still you go back to your thieving ways. There is only one thing left and if that does not work, then it will be St. Savlons for you, young man."

"Oh not St. Savlons, please Mam. My Courtleigh is a good boy at heart," Gran pleaded. "He's been brought up properly. I've always told him not to take things from shops." She turned towards her grandson. "You know that's not how you do it, Courtleigh."

"I tried to put something back," he muttered.

"Excuse me!" Mrs Whiteside cried. "I am not accustomed to being interrupted in my own court. What is all this nonsense about putting things back? He should never have taken anything in the first place!"

Gran drew herself up to her full four foot ten and looked steadily at the magistrate. "The way it goes Mam is this. You never take but you also give."

"And what is that supposed to mean?" snapped Mrs Whiteside.

"Let me explain," Gran said softly. "It's like this…" and she began to talk in a low, dark voice, that was like treacle dripping off a spoon, so soothing and calming that Mrs Whiteside felt herself growing sleepy and finding it harder and harder to concentrate on what was being said. She had fully intended to send this criminally minded teenager straight into youth custody, but by the time Gran had finished, she was thinking of foster care with weekends home for good behaviour.

"Mr and Mrs Harris are very experienced, especially with the more difficult sort of child," she said. "But let me warn you Courtleigh, one step out of line and it will be straight to St. Savlons."

"Thank you Mam. I am sure he will behave. Won't you Courtleigh?"

Courtleigh said nothing. He didn't want to leave his Gran. He didn't want to live in a foster home. But what could he do?

CHAPTER TWO

"It wasn't me." Polly Miller looked straight at her social worker. "I didn't do it."

Jenny Abramawitch raised her eyebrows. She was young and as bright as an autumn leaf. Her eyes behind her round glasses were very green. "That's what you always say Polly. You are eleven years old, you have been in care all your life and this has happened how many times?"

"It's not my fault, if I haven't got a mum or dad." Polly was determined to change the subject and talking about her family always worked, even with Miss Abramawitch. "I couldn't help it, if they got killed when the fire work factory blew up."

"That's not necessarily true. No one knows exactly what happened that night." Jenny's hands fluttered over the piles of paper on the desk. "A woman was seen not far from where you were found. She was bleeding badly, but she wandered away before anyone could help her."

"That wasn't my mum. My mum wouldn't have left me."

"I'm sure she wouldn't have if she knew what she was doing, but people do strange things when they're in shock," Jenny said gently.

Polly shrugged. What did it matter if no one knew? No one cared. No one wanted her. She was on her own and that's how she would always be. She lifted her chin and stared out of the window. She was a squarish sort of girl with mousy brown hair cut in a ragged fringe. She wore a pair of faded jeans, a stained and matted jumper and scuffed trainers.

"This latest fire, I suppose it could have been an accident," Jenny said hopefully.

"There were rosebuds all over the walls and the sheets," Polly muttered.

"Mrs. Brown was only trying to make your room pretty for you."

"I hate pretty," Polly scowled.

"So you got out the matches?"

"No I didn't. I told you, I didn't do it. It just sort of happened."

Jenny Abramawitch shook her head. "It's beginning to happen more and more often," she said softly. "Ever since you were little there have been fires. Let's see, there was the one when I left you at the nursery, though that could have been the gas heater exploding. Then you went to a school you didn't like and the oil tank leaked all over the playground and somehow a match was dropped and there was a rather unfortunate explosion. Last year there was that chip pan fire. I know you were nowhere near the kitchen at the time, so I suppose you couldn't be blamed, but later that month the fireworks for Bonfire Night blew up and the sofa caught fire and then last night at Mrs. Brown's the bedroom burst into flames."

Polly said nothing. She kicked the rucksack that lay at her feet. It was made of old green webbing and she had for as long as she could remember. Inside were her really important things and some spare clothes, a towel and a toothbrush, in case she had to leave in a hurry.

"Well," said Jenny. "What am I going to do with you?" She pushed back her chair and leaned over to pick up Polly's folder. It was so full and heavy that she had to wrap both her arms around it. Wedges of paper squidged out like ketchup from a hot dog. Jenny Abramawitch tapped the cover with her nail. "In here Polly are the details of all the foster homes you've been to and all the reasons why you had to leave."

Polly stuck out her lower lip. "I don't care," she muttered.

"Well you should," Jenny said firmly, her eyes glinting behind her glasses.

Under the table, Polly scuffed the toes of her trainers against the floor. These things kept happening to her. Maybe one day they'd stop, or maybe they wouldn't, but by then she'd be grown up and could live somewhere where it didn't matter.

"Listen Polly, you've got one last chance. If this doesn't work out, then it's St. Savlons."

Polly's stomach flipped up towards her throat. Her fingers closed around the dried up piece of twig she wore on a shoe lace around her neck. It was her lucky charm. She'd been holding it, when she was found in the ruins of the Duke Street flats.

Jenny Abramawitch scooped up the papers and pushed them back into the folder. Then she stood up and put her bag on the desk. It was made of patchwork with bamboo handles and was as big as a suitcase. From it she took a length of marmalade coloured ribbon, which she bound tightly round the folder before placing it into the bottom of the bag. "Come on Polly let's give it a go. And this time, please try to behave."

Polly picked up her rucksack and shrugged it over her shoulders. She thrust her hands into her pockets and followed Jenny out of her office. She'd been there so many times, she no longer noticed the sludge green walls and stained brown carpet.

As the door shut behind them, a sleek cream cat with blue eyes and pale purple ears, twined itself round Jenny's legs. "Are you coming with us, Lucy?" Jenny asked.

The cat considered. She looked from one to the other, then holding her tail like an exclamation mark, she led the way to the car park. When she got to the little red car, she waited purring impatiently, while Jenny rummaged in her bag for the keys.

Polly fastened her seat belt and crossed her fingers. The car leapt forward and kangarooed down the High Street, then puffed and snorted its way along Acacia Avenue before skidding past the children's playground and down the hill into the fearsome Southwold estate. They juddered past houses, whose windows were boarded up, shops with shutters made of steel and walls sprayed with graffiti. Polly scowled. She'd lived here before and she didn't like it.

Suddenly, she felt the wiry touch of a whisker on her cheek, as Lucy leaned forward and placed a paw on Jenny's shoulder. The car lurched to a halt. Jenny Abramawitch rolled down the window. "Courtleigh," she called.

The boy glanced over his shoulder, but there was nowhere to run. Instead of his school uniform he wore big baggy trousers, a large yellow T shirt, huge trainers with their tongues hanging out and a baseball cap back to front. He had skin the colour of palest chocolate and eyes like velvet.

"Yes Mam."

"Shouldn't you be at school?"

"Yes Mam."

"Then what are you doing in Wilmot Drive?"

"Why walking Mam."

"To school?"

Courtleigh grinned. "Could be," he said.

Jenny Abramawitch raised her eyes and gave a big sigh. "Get in."

Courtleigh opened the door, looked at Polly and spread out his hands. "I don't think there's room," he said.

"Oh no you don't. Polly get in the back." Polly looked reluctantly at the back seat, but she did as she was told, for there was something about Jenny Abramawitch that made it very difficult to disobey. As she slid in beside the cat, Lucy raised her head from her paws and slowly and elegantly settled herself on Polly's lap and began to purr.

Jenny Abramawitch turned the key and crashed the gears. The engine coughed and shuddered, Jenny took her hands off the wheel and said, "It's lucky we met you Courtleigh. Not only did we pick you up before you got yourself into any more trouble, but we're all going to the same place. Like you, Polly is going to live with Mr and Mrs Harris."

Courtleigh turned and looked at Polly, his face grim. "Bad luck kid," he said softly.

CHAPTER THREE

At the top of Gibbons Way the car stalled. Jenny Abramawitch looked anxiously from side to side, then turned the key and stamped on the accelerator. They shot past a row of neat little houses with well kept gardens and slammed to a halt in front of number 49.

"We're here," she announced.

Courtleigh sighed softly and Polly bit her lip. The house was twice the size of any other in the street. The extensions, which Mr Harris had added to every possible roof and wall, made it look top heavy and about to tumble into the garden on top of the four rusting cars, the concrete mixer and the dog kennel with the name Brutus tacked on to its roof.

"It will be all right. Really it will," Jenny Abramawitch said. Courtleigh made a rude noise at the back of his throat.

"They always say that when it's something nasty," Polly muttered.

"Out you get." No one moved. "Now please," there was a hint of steel in Jenny's voice and a glint in her green eyes.

Courtleigh unfolded himself from the car. He pulled his baseball cap over his eyes and glowered. Lucy gave an indignant mew and slid off Polly's lap straight into the patchwork bag her mistress held open for her.

"She'll suffocate," Polly said.

"She'll be safe," Jenny replied. There was a ferocious barking and a huge black dog charged out of the kennel. Only the chain attached to his collar stopped him attacking. "He won't hurt you," Jenny's voice trembled, as she tried to sound confident.

"Oh no," Polly said sarcastically, backing away from the furious animal.

"No problem," Courtleigh drawled. He pushed back his cap and swaggered up to the creature. Polly half shut her eyes and waited for him to be torn to pieces, but as he stretched out his hand and murmured something under his breath, the growling stopped and the dog gazed up at him in adoration. Courtleigh scratched his ears and Brutus turned over and waggled his paws in the air. Keeping as far from the dog as she could, Jenny Abramawitch hurried up the front steps and rang the bell.

The girl, who opened the door, had sleek blonde hair and bright gold nail varnish. She was dressed in skin tight jeans and was holding an electric eyelash curler in her hand.

"Mum," she called. "It's Miss A with the new girl." At the end of the hall a door banged and a woman appeared. She was small and thin and her long nose and tight bright curls gave her the look of an anxious mouse.

"Shoes," she squeaked. Jenny lifted her skirt to reveal a pair of tightly laced boots. "Oh not you, Miss A." Mrs Harris darted a meaningful glance at Courtleigh. "As you can see we've just had new carpets and Mr Harris has papered the hall and the landing. It's all new and all paid for."

Polly glanced around at the swirling patterns of pink and lilac, which made her think of something that had been squashed on the road. Courtleigh leaned back against the salmon and purple wall and slowly and deliberately shuffled off his trainers. He picked them up and swinging them by the laces carried them up the stairs. Mrs Harris watched until he reached the landing.

"Boys! What would you do with them?" she sighed. "Now if you'd like to come along into the kitchen, it's more friendly."

The kitchen was white and dazzling. Anything that was not white was stainless steel and every surface was crammed with electrical equipment. There was a television, a stereo, two microwaves, a coffee maker, a kettle, a mixer, a juicer, a blender, an electric carving knife, an ice cream maker and a machine for crunching up ice cubes.

"All new and all paid for," Mrs Harris said proudly. "Sit yourselves down." She pointed to the round white table and spindly chairs. "I'll just call Mr Harris. He's in the back doing something with the satellite dish. He's fixed it so we get two hundred and forty channels. Very clever with anything electrical Mr Harris is. Rewired the whole house himself, you know." She wiped her hands down her nylon overall, opened the back door and called, "Jerry!"

Mr Harris was short, with a bald head and red face. His arms and shoulders were thick with muscles and his belly hung over his trousers. He was wearing a string vest and through it Polly could see the names, Jerry and Janice tattooed on either side of his chest.

"Is this the little girl then?" He squinted at Polly and shook his head. "She doesn't look like a problem to me."

"She isn't," Jenny said a little too quickly. "But she's had a number of different foster homes. She's found it," she paused, "hard to settle," she said finally.

Mr Harris slapped his forehead. "I know. Feels unloved most like. Still we can deal with that, can't we love?" He turned to look at his wife. A little pinkness crept into her cheeks.

"Of course we can. We do our best with all our children."

"You've had a lot of experience," Jenny's voice was a little weak and she kept her eyes away from Polly, who was staring hard at the floor, determined not to let anyone see how bad she was feeling.

"Eight of our own and how many others is it now?" Mrs Harris turned to her husband.

"Twenty five, over the years. And never a bit of trouble from any of them," he said, proudly. Jenny fluttered to her feet.

"Now that's settled, I have to be going. I've got another urgent case to deal with today. Goodbye Polly." Suddenly and unexpectedly, she bent and gave her a kiss. "Be good. It really is for the best," she whispered. Polly felt the drop of a tear on her cheek, then Jenny Abramawitch was gone.

"Don't you fret," Mr Harris put his hand on Polly's shoulder. "You'll soon feel at home here. One big happy family that's what we are." Gently he guided Polly into a seat. "We're here to help you to be the best you can be."

"If there's anything bothering you, you've only got to say," Mrs Harris murmured. They both looked expectantly at her. Polly shuffled her feet on the floor.

"We know you've had a difficult time," Mr Harris prompted. There was a long pause. Polly kicked at the tiles with her toes.

"Can I go to my room?" she said at last. Her foster parents exchanged glances.

"Not ready to talk yet," Mrs Harris said.

Not ready to talk ever, Polly thought.

"We'll get one of the girls to show you where everything is," Mr Harris said kindly. "Make you feel welcome, like."

"I'm Jemma," the girl, with the gold nails said as she led the way up the puce and lavender stairs.

"Oh yeah," Polly said carelessly.

"That's Jasmine and Jade's room," Jemma waved her hand at an open door. "They've got a plasma screen and a music centre and there are gold taps in their en-suite. But that's because they're older than me. That's our room," she continued and Polly stopped and gazed in horror at sugar pink walls and two mini four poster beds draped in white muslin. "No. That's not yours," Jemma smiled kindly at her mistake. "It's mine and Jodie's. Jason, Josh, Jimbo and Darren are in the new extension. They've got a pool table in there. Here," she opened a white painted door, which led to a plain wooden staircase. "You're up there."

There were two doors at the top, one of which was firmly shut. From behind it Polly heard the faint sounds of the Test Match.

"Courtleigh," Jemma shrugged. "He likes cricket!" her voice rose in disbelief. "You're in here."

To Polly's relief the small attic room was painted white. There was a single bed, a chair and chest of drawers, above which hung a huge cork notice board.

"That's for your stars," Jemma explained, settling herself on the bed. "You get them for being the best you can be. I've nearly got enough for my own TV and Jason's going to get his car next week. Jas's already got hers."

"Mm," Polly grunted and dumped her rucksack on the end of the bed.

"Is that all you've brought?" Jemma shrieked. Polly shot her a dark look, but she   continued. "It's OK. You can borrow some of my stuff.

16

I've got loads. I got a leather jacket last week and now I've got enough stars for my designer jeans. Good or what?" she stood up and smoothed her hands down her legs. Polly glowered. "I'll get Jade to do your nails for you if you like," Jemma offered. "She's really good at it. Look." She waved her hand in front of Polly's face.

Polly's eyes narrowed. There was a faint stir of air; a gathering of dust from under the bed; a flicker of curtains moved by an unseen breeze.

"Are you sure…?" Jemma began.

"Yep," Polly said decisively. "I don't do nails." The twig round her neck swung heavily on its piece of string and the room darkened with menace. Jemma backed rapidly out of the door and staggered down the stairs as fast as she could in her spindly sandals.

CHAPTER FOUR

"At least it's not rosebuds," Polly muttered. She rubbed her eyes fiercely and sat down on the bed. Another house, another place where she did not belong. Another family, who got on together, even if they all had stupid names beginning with J. Except for Darren. She tried a watery giggle. The door across the landing opened.

"You're not unpacking?" Courtleigh said. Polly sighed.

"I suppose I've got to," she said.

"It's not that bad."

"No?"

"They just try to understand you. You know, find out why you do the things you do. You get used to it."

"I don't think so," Polly said. She didn't understand the things she did, so how could anyone else? "How long have you been here then?"

"Six months," Courtleigh said briefly. Polly wanted to know more. Why was he in care? What had happened to his family? But she wasn't sure Courtleigh wanted to tell her, so she said nothing. They were quiet for a bit, then Polly said,

"Miss A says if I'm bad this time, it's…"

"St. Savlons," Courtleigh finished.

"You too?"

"Me too."

There was another silence, as they both thought of the horror of St.Savlons.

"They say no one ever comes out of there. Once you're in, you're never seen again," Polly said at last.

"That's not true, I know some kids…" Courtleigh began.

"Courtleigh, Polly football in the back yard," a voice floated up the stairs.

Courtleigh groaned and screwed up his face. "Oh man, that's Jason. He gets stars for organizing a game. So we…"

"Can be the best we can be," Polly giggled. "Come on," she jumped off the bed. Courtleigh did not move. "You coming?" she prompted.

"Nah. West Indies are playing."

"OK. See you."

Polly ran down the stairs. She loved playing football. In her last school she'd been in the school team. It had taken some persuading, but the PE teacher had finally agreed and she'd scored the winning goal in their last match against St. Edwards. Remembering how the ball had slammed into the back of the net, she thrust her arms into the air and leapt down the last two steps.

"You coming to watch?" Jemma slid her arm through Polly's.

"What do I want to do that for?" With a practiced wriggle Polly slipped free. "I'm playing."

"You can't do that!" Jemma was horrified.

"Why not?" Polly asked.

"We don't do football," Jemma tried to explain. "It's only for boys." Polly stared at her in amazement. "We're the crowd. We got our teams," Jemma continued. "We got to support them. Cheer and things."

"Boring," Polly chanted.

"Dad says…" Jemma began, but Polly did not want to hear what Mr Harris had to say on the subject of girls playing football.

Ignoring Jemma's protests, she ran out into the back garden, which had been turned into a football pitch, by the addition of two goals at either end of what had once been a lawn. Four blonde boys, of varying ages, were kicking a ball about. Three blonde girls perched on the patio wall, chatting and giggling and when Polly appeared Jasmine, the eldest waved her over.

"Budge up Jodie and you Jade," she said to her sisters, who shuffled along obediently to make room for two more spectators. Jemma slid in between them. Polly charged straight onto the pitch.

"What's she doing?" Jade cried.

"I dunno. I think she's gone mad," Jemma bit her lip. "See!"

Jason was passing to Jimbo, Josh tackled his brother and got possession; racing down the pitch, he lined up the ball and was about to shoot, when out of nowhere came a small squarish body. Dodging past Darren, she slid under Josh's guard and the ball was hers.

"Hey!" Darren yelled. He dived at Polly and arms round her waist in a rugby tackle wrestled her to the floor.

"Get off me," she hissed. Darren grinned and sat down hard on her legs. Polly twisted herself round. She tried punching him, but he leaned sideways and she couldn't reach him.

"It was my ball," he taunted. Polly lay still. "And you're not playing," his face loomed over hers. She waited, then reared up and bit him hard on the ear.

"Dad!" Darren shrieked, stumbling to his feet. "Jas," he sobbed as the blood dripped down his neck.

"Polly what have you done?" Mr Harris trundled out of the house. "Jason take Darren inside and see to him. Polly you're coming with me."

"No I'm not," Polly dug her heels into the muddy ground. "I'm not going anywhere. It wasn't my fault," she said loudly, in case anyone was unsure. "I didn't do anything."

"Dad she bit him," Jasmine cried. "She went wild."

"Polly," Mr Harris shook his head sorrowfully. "Come on there's a good girl."

"Won't," Polly said. She knew she was making things worse, but she didn't care. It was Darren who should be getting into trouble, not her. Mr Harris sighed heavily.

"Jimbo, Josh give me a hand."

"No," Polly cried, but it was too late. Jimbo took one arm, Josh the other and however hard she kicked and struggled, she could not break free. Grimly the Harris boys led her into the kitchen and sat her down at the white table. One stood behind her, the other held onto her arms as Mr Harris lowered himself into a spindly chair and looked at her sorrowfully.

"Polly, Polly," he said. "This is not the way to do it. This is not being the best you can be."

"It wasn't my fault," Polly repeated. "He fouled me."

"And you bit him."

"Yeah, well, he wouldn't let me go." She glared defiantly around the pristine white room. "It's Darren who wasn't being the best he could be," she said.

"You attacked him," Mr Harris said very slowly, as if she was too stupid to understand. "You must say sorry."

"Why? I told you what happened. Why should I say sorry and not him?"

"Because what you did was wrong and if you can't see that, then I'm very sorry."

"It wasn't just me," Polly's voice was rising.

"I know how you must be feeling," Mr Harris ignored her protest. "And I'm afraid," he paused and for a terrible moment Polly thought she was going to be sent straight to St. Savlons, "we'll have to put a minus on your star chart. But I'm sure you'll try to do better tomorrow."

"Won't," Polly muttered.

"Then I'm sorry, but you'll have to go to your room and stay there until you're ready to be part of this family."

I'll never be that, Polly thought furiously, as Mr Harris marched her to her room and shut the door.

Sitting down on the bed, fists clenched, she stared at the blank wall and tried not to think about what might happen next. There was a quick tap on the door and Courtleigh came in.

"What's up?"

"Nothing," Polly scuffed her feet on the floorboards.

"OK," Courtleigh turned as if he was going and suddenly she did not want to be left on her own.

"I was only trying to play," she muttered.

"What did you do?" Courtleigh sat down beside her.

"I bit Darren on the ear," she said. "He was sitting on my legs," she added hastily.

"Hey man," Courtleigh grinned. "You bit that spoiled brat. You should wash your mouth out, or he might poison you."

"Ugh," Polly pretended to spit and they both laughed. They sat there companionably for a while, then she said, "I hate them. I hate those stupid Js."

Courtleigh shrugged. "It's not that bad," he said.

Polly thought of other foster homes she had been in. "I suppose," she admitted finally.

"You gonna say you're sorry then?"

"No."

"You may as well."

"No. I won't. Never. Not even if I have to stay in my room for the rest of my life. It was NOT my fault."

A delicious smell floated up the stairs. "Polly, Courtleigh, we've got Chinese," Jade called. Courtleigh looked at Polly. She shook her head.

"I'm not saying it."

"But…"

"You go. I'm not saying sorry. Never." Hugging her empty stomach, Polly turned her back on him and scowled at the wall. She heard him clatter down the stairs; heard the sound of voices; Jemma and the girls shrieking in disbelief; Mr Harris sounding sad and disappointed. Then a door shut and there was silence. Her insides growled and rumbled. Rocking slightly on her heels she reached up and twisted the piece of string she wore round her neck. The rough texture was soothing, the feel of the twig familiar and somehow comforting. In spite of her hunger, her eyes began to close.

"Polly," Courtleigh's voice broke through her half sleep. "I've brought you some supper. Here, move over man. I've got chicken in black bean sauce, sweet and sour pork, lemon chicken and fried rice."

"What, no stir fry veg?" Grinning Polly made room for him. "Thanks. I'm starving."

"They'd have left you 'til breakfast time," Courtleigh said as they ate. "That's what it's like here. They reckon you're the one that has to decide to …"

"I know," Polly licked soya sauce smeared fingers, "be the best you can." She pulled a face. "What if you're the best already and don't want to be any better? Then what do you do?"

Courtleigh shrugged. "Dunno. I'm going to get rid of these cartons, then watch some serious cricket." He gathered up the packaging and was moving towards the door, when suddenly he stopped and groaned, "Oh man."

"Courtleigh Jones, I am so disappointed in you." Mr Harris, red faced and panting, appeared at the top of the stairs. "It's up to Polly to decide when she's ready to come and eat. You know the rules of the house and you know the consequences."

Courtleigh hung his head. "Yes sir," he mumbled.

"There's only one privilege you have left," Mr Harris said heavily. Courtleigh clamped his lips together and nodded. "Jason," Mr Harris called. "Come and get Courtleigh's TV."

"That's not fair," Polly leapt from the bed. "Tell him Courtleigh. Tell him."

Courtleigh said nothing. Shoulders slumped, he walked into his bedroom and shut the door. "You can't do this," Polly yelled at Mr Harris, who shook his head and said kindly,

"It's the rules. You'll learn. It feels cruel, but believe me it's for your own good and Courtleigh's too of course."

It isn't, it isn't, it isn't, Polly thought pacing up and down the room. *It's only what grown ups say when they know they're wrong. I hate them, I hate them all.* She sank down on the floor and leaned her back against the bed. It was so unfair. Courtleigh had only wanted to help her and now he had lost something that was really important to him. She wished she could get up and knock on his door and say she was sorry. She was sorry he couldn't watch his cricket, but she wasn't sorry that she refused to apologize to Darren. That would mean giving in to Mr Harris and playing his stupid games and she was never ever going to do that. Never.

CHAPTER FIVE

Polly lay on her bed, angry and miserable. She hadn't bothered to undress. There was no point; she wasn't going to sleep, not with all this churning through her brain. She hated the Harrises. Because of their stupid ideas, Courtleigh wouldn't be her friend. She didn't blame him, if he never spoke to her again. Polly let out a long and furious breath. It would be like it always was. Polly Miller alone against the rest of the world.

In the airing cupboard, the heater gave a funny little hiccough. A stereo switched itself on then off, then on again. Steam rose from the electric kettle and the microwave pinged. A light bulb glowed brightly, then shattered, sprinkling glass all over the pink and purple carpet.

About midnight the first wisp of smoke uncoiled itself from the wiring. It rose lazily to the ceiling, where it looped a few loops, then hung around for a while, until it remembered what it was meant to do and burst into flames.

In the bedroom over the garage, Darren Harris couldn't breathe. He thought one of his brothers was holding a pillow over his face, but when he opened his eyes, he saw smoke billowing in under the door.

"Fire!" he screamed, rolling off the bunk bed and kicking and thumping his brothers, until they woke up.

"Get your stuff out," Jason ordered.

"Should we shout Mum and Dad?" Darren asked.

"They've got the alarm. They'll be OK. You get yourself out," Josh said and laden with televisions, keyboards, guitars, computers and as many of their possessions as they could carry, they hurried down the emergency stairs their dad had fixed onto the end of the extension.

When they reached the garden, they found Mrs Harris screaming for her boys, and the girls screeching to their friends on their mobiles.

"That fire alarm should have gone off. It cost a bomb and an arm and a leg," Mr. Harris muttered, mournfully shaking his head.

The fire engines roared down Gibbons Road. Brutus howled and neighbours came running out into the street to watch the Harris' house burn down. No one gave a thought to the two children trapped in the attic.

Polly watched the flames licking the edge of the curtains. She liked the way the thin grey material blossomed into plumes of scarlet and orange. Soon there would be touches of blue and green, but it was getting hotter and she hadn't got time to wait. Somehow she had known this was going to happen. Grabbing her rucksack, she made for the door, but when she opened it, she saw that the stairs were alight and there was no way down. Polly's stomach flipped and her legs went weak, then Courtleigh's hand was on her elbow.

"This way," he said pushing open the landing window. The sudden rush of air drew the flames roaring up the staircase and Polly could feel the heat on the back of her neck.

"It's too high to jump," she cried.

"There's a drain pipe outside. Hold on and slide. Now."

Polly's head was through the window, her hands round the pipe, but the plastic surface was slippery, her fingers were losing their grip and she was falling head first, straight down into the concrete yard. There was nothing she could do. Polly closed her eyes. Her lucky charm bumped up against her throat. The ground was coming closer and closer, she could feel it rushing towards her, she was not going to look, she was not...

"Get off!" Something soft and squidgey was beating her on the head. Polly sat up and opened her eyes. Whatever it was scuttled to its feet. In the moonlight, she thought it looked like a cushion with feet, then as it stared back at her, she decided it was more like a cross between a moth eaten teddy bear and a large rat. "Watch it 'ere comes another one."

Polly rolled to one side and Courtleigh fell through the gap in the concrete and landed beside her. She saw flames leaping into the sky and beyond them a pattern of stars. Then darkness, as the hole closed over.

She fumbled for her rucksack and pulled out her torch. She was sitting on a pile of rubbish, in what looked like a cave, except that the walls were made of brick.

Courtleigh sat up and rubbed the back of his head. "Wow," he said. "I found it. I found the way in."

"What?" Polly looked at him warily. Had the fall scrambled his brain?

"I found the key," Courtleigh continued triumphantly. "It's what Gran tried to teach me," he explained earnestly to the bemused Polly. "She said if ever things got real bad and I had to hide out, I was to go down to The Edges."

"Is this where we are now?" she asked, pretending to believe he was making sense. She knew that when someone had a knock on the head, you had to be very careful with them, in case they got violent.

"I guess." Courtleigh grinned broadly.

"The Edges of what?" Polly said.

"I don't know." Courtleigh shrugged, looking puzzled. Polly began to back away.

There was a rustling and a scrabbling and the small furry creature advanced, its paws on its hips.

"This is the Edge of Things," he said firmly. Polly and Courtleigh stared in amazement. "You shouldn't be 'ere. This is no place for 'umans."

"It was an emergency," Courtleigh faltered.

"Be that as it may, you still got to go. Lucky for you, you've got me,

30

Podner, to show you the way. I'm the best and I know all the ways up and down. All you've got to do is follow."

"What if we don't want to?" Courtleigh said.

"You don't 'ave no choice." The creature drew his eyes together. He snarled and his fur stood on end. Polly bit her lip to stop herself laughing out loud. He looked like an angry fur ball and was so small, that she could easily have picked him up and thrown him over the top of the rubbish. "My teeth are very sharp," Podner growled.

"Yeah man." Courtleigh caught Polly's eye and grinned.

"I'm the best," Podner said menacingly, making a lunge at Polly's ankles. In the light of the torch his teeth looked suddenly very big and yellow and fierce.

"OK. We'll go," Courtleigh put his hands up in surrender and Podner's fur flattened.

"That's all right then. I'll lead, you follow and keep close. There's things down 'ere you don't want to see and don't want to see you neither. Get a move on. We 'aven't got all day." He gave a self important little swagger, then scrambled over a pile of rotting newspapers, black and slimy with mould, kicked aside a drift of dry leaves and set off down the tunnel. Polly hoisted her rucksack over her shoulders and holding the torch steady, she and Courtleigh followed.

The brick passageway was low and narrow. In some places Courtleigh had to bend his head to stop it touching the roof. Polly being much smaller had no problem, but she kept stopping to make sure he was alright. Podner, on the other hand, trotted so fast, that at times he was almost out of the reach of the torch and all they could see was a fat little shadow at the very edge of the beam.

Gradually the tunnel grew wider. The ground was still paved, but the walls were made of earth. Polly stopped suddenly. "There are houses buried down here," she gasped. "Look you can see their shapes."

"Cool." Courtleigh ran his hand over the outline of a window sill. The earth crumbled and fell in a heap at his feet. Beneath it was a thick slab of stone.

"Leave it be," Podner snapped. He peered anxiously from side to side, his ears standing up on the top of his head, as if he were listening for something far off in the distance.

"It must be really old," Polly said, ignoring him.

"From the beginning," Podner snarled.

"The beginning of what?"

"Of the Kingdoms, of course."

"I thought we were in The Edges."

"We are." Podner gave a huge sigh. "Don't you know nothing?"

"Not about down here."

"Well you wouldn't, I suppose, being 'uman. They've gone their way and we've..." A roar like the coming of a train drowned the rest of his words. Podner's fur shot up in terror. The tunnel shook. "Come on, we've got to get out of 'ere." The noise grew louder, a rumbling sound like thunder filled the tunnel, bouncing from the walls and echoing in their heads. "There's got to be one 'ere somewhere," Podner gasped. He ran frantically up and down sniffing.

"What are we looking for?" Polly said.

"The door of course. What do you think? We've got to get out," Podner said desperately.

"Stay cool. We'll find it. Try over there, Polly." Polly shone the torch over the window that Courtleigh had found. "There's something here." Courtleigh began pulling at a root growing out of the stonework. The earth fell away, revealing a doorway.

"They're 'ere. It's too late. We'll be crushed," Podner cried.

Behind them, a huge white machine, blocked the entrance to the tunnel. Square in shape, its windows were black as night. Courtleigh pushed against the door. The wood began to give. The machine hissed, square metallic flaps opened and four white hoses snaked towards them.

"Out of the way." Courtleigh hurled himself at the door. The ancient wood crumbled, leaving just enough room to squeeze through. Polly picked up Podner and threw him at the gap, she went next, followed by Courtleigh's head, his shoulders, his waist and then, "It's got my foot," he yelled.

"Kick your trainers off," Polly cried.

"No way. They're brand new." The top half of his body shook, as he kicked out at the machine. But it was too strong for him. Bit by bit it was pulling him back.

"Courtleigh," Polly yelled.

It was too late. He was gone.

CHAPTER SIX

Polly stared at the place in the tunnel wall, where Courtleigh's head had been.

"The Scooper's got 'im," Podner said.

"We've got to do something," she cried furiously. "We can't leave him like that. I'm going to get him."

"No you don't. That's my job." Podner darted past her and dived straight through the gap in the wall. Polly heard a shout followed by a slurp and a hiss, then Podner was back and after him came Courtleigh, skimming the ground like a surfer on a board, as he threw himself out of the reach of the Scooper.

"Are you OK?" Polly said anxiously.

Courtleigh sat up and rubbed his bruised toes. "What did you do that for?"

"If I 'adn't bitten your laces, it would 'ave got you," Podner said huffily.

"But those were my new trainers," Courtleigh mourned. "What did it want them for anyway?"

"'Ow should I know. It scoops things up. That's what it does. You was lucky you was with me, otherwise it would 'ave got you for sure."

"No it wouldn't. Courtleigh's too big for it." Polly looked at Podner, who would easily fit into one of the Scooper's hoses and had risked being caught to save a boy he did not even know. "You were brave."

"I told you. I'm the best," Podner said proudly. "Now get a move on, before it decides to clean up down this way."

"As soon as we're out of here, I'm off to Gran's," Courtleigh said. "Got to get me some shoes. Where's the way out?"

"Follow me and I'll show you. And 'urry up before anything else 'appens."

Podner led them into a wide tunnel, where, through the gloom, skeletons of houses could be seen on either side of a cobbled street. "Come on," he growled, as Polly stopped to stare at a broken archway. Half buried in the soil, above it she could see a crest showing two dragons with their necks entwined breathing fire.

"Is this all part of the old Kingdoms?" she began.

"I told you, there's no time to gawp." Podner bared his teeth.

"But I want to know," Polly protested, then skipped quickly out of the way as Podner dived at her ankles. Snapping and snarling he herded her down the tunnel, until they came to a narrow gap way between two houses.

"The quickest way is back through 'ere. And that's where you're

36

going. And no more questions, or I'll bite."

They stumbled into the passage way. Polly went first. It was dark and musty and they had to feel their way by holding on to the walls. It grew narrower and narrower, until the sides were grazing Courtleigh's shoulders. He couldn't see. He stuck his arms out and something sticky and clingy twisted round his fingers. It pressed over his eyes and his ears, winding itself round his nose and reaching down into his lungs. Coughing and spluttering, he blundered through the curtain of spiders' webs and spat out a gob of spider silk.

"That went on my fur!" Podner yelped.

"Sorry," Courtleigh choked. "Couldn't help it." He rubbed his eyes clear. On the other side of the passage the walls were tiled and there was a glimmer of light in the distance.

A very aggrieved Podner was sitting on the ground pulling bits of web from his coat. Suddenly he gave a shriek and covered his face with his paws, as a white figure came lurching towards them. It had no eyes or face and it was moaning and searching blindly for its prey. Courtleigh took a deep breath and started to back away. The thing began to quiver and shake, then burst into a scatter of giggles.

"Good thing, I'm not scared of spiders," Polly said, as she pulled the towel from her head. "Not like you two."

"We're not," Courtleigh cried.

Polly grinned and stuffed her towel back in her rucksack. "I can smell trains," she said, her voice echoing round the white tiled walls of the tunnel.

"Cool man, just show us the exit."

Podner nodded briskly, then his ears stood up on the top of his head and his nose quivered.

"Stay cool, there's nothing coming."

"There is. Listen." Polly held up her hand and they heard the first faint rumble of the Scooper.

"Run," Podner squeaked. He set off, his paws slapping against stone, until suddenly he swerved to the right and disappeared. Courtleigh skidded to a halt.

"He's gone."

"He can't have."

"I can't see him."

"Nor can I." Polly peered into the dimness. "Where is he?" She was just about to shout his name, when Courtleigh pointed to a smooth dark patch on the tiles.

"It's another tunnel." They retraced their steps, made a sharp turn and found themselves in a soft earthy dimness.

"What kept you? I said you was to follow me." Podner's voice came querulously out of the gloom.

They plodded on. Polly rubbed the sleep out of her eyes and thought longingly of a soft warm bed. Courtleigh imagined breakfast at Gran's.

A plate brimming with ackees, bacon, tomatoes and Johnny cakes. He scuffed his feet wearily and kicked up a cloud of sand. It hung in the air for a moment, then like a tiny tornado, it whirled past and was swallowed by the thick white tube snaking towards them.

They ran. The tunnel twisted and turned. The soft surface dragged at their legs pulling them down and making it harder and harder to move. Behind them they could hear the growl of the Scooper and the hiss of the hoses. Desperately they looked for somewhere to hide, but there were no nooks or crannies, nothing but blank walls and a faint ray of light spilling out from beneath a purple front door.

"We're saved!" Polly banged on the glossy paint.

There was a wheezing sound, then a faint breathless voice, quavered, "Oh do come in." The door swung open and they half fell into a bower of shimmering delight. Candles burned in holders made from cans, tins and bottles. Ribbons of silver, blue, red and green foil, sparkled in the light; some were pressed into the walls, others hung from wires suspended from the ceiling. Shards of coloured glass made up a fake window. Purple silk cushions were heaped on the floor and on the biggest one sprawled a thin pale dragon. Its eyes were closed, one claw rested on its forehead, the other held an inhaler up to its nose.

"Forgive me. It's my lungs," the dragon wheezed. It breathed in deeply, then relaxed. "I promise you, the air down here is getting worse and worse," it opened a pale eye. "Oh how very rude of me. Where are my manners?"

"I'm sorry. We didn't mean to burst in, but it was an emergency," Polly said.

The dragon waved a paw. "No, no you don't understand." It gave a great sigh. Its whole body began to shake, the pale skin grew paler and paler, until it was almost invisible, but just before it disappeared completely, it took the shape of a thin, young man with white blonde hair, very pale skin and long dark eye lashes. "That's better," he said, taking a deep breath from his inhaler.

Polly blinked. Was it the candle light or was she seeing things? She looked at Courtleigh, who shrugged his shoulders. "Shape changer," he whispered. "Gran told me about them."

The young man waved his hands about. "Come in; sit down; make yourselves at home. It's delightful to see you. It's simply eons since I had a visit from the upper regions, which is probably why I have completely forgotten how to behave. Let me introduce myself. I am Jocelyn von Drakenberg and who are you?"

"Courtleigh Jones."

"The Joneses of West London or the Joneses of Carmarthen?"

Courtleigh shrugged, not knowing what to answer and Jocelyn half closed his eyes and surveyed him from under his lashes.

"Mm I think not. More like the Joneses of Trench Town. And you?" He turned to Polly, but before she could reply, something hard hit her on the knee. She glared down at Podner.

"What did you do that for?" she hissed.

"Me! I didn't do nothing," Podner said innocently.

"Oh what a cutie." As Jocelyn leaned down to look at Podner, Polly caught the smell of brimstone on his breath and without thinking, put her hand up to her nose.

"Don't worry I'm not going to bite," he said huffily. "Speaking of which, you two must be simply starving. Do let me find you something to eat."

Polly shook her head. Podner, who was eager to leave, tugged at her jeans, but Courtleigh was hungry. "Great. Thanks," he said.

"Won't be a tick." Jocelyn went to the back of the cave and disappeared behind a curtain made from bottle tops threaded onto silver wire.

"He's probably making an ash sandwich, or mixing up a paraffin shake," Polly said crossly.

"Don't be stupid, when he's human, he's got to eat like humans," Courtleigh said.

"So long as he doesn't eat humans," Polly said sulkily.

"Stupid." Courtleigh swung a mock punch at her. Polly side stepped and not looking where she was going, trod on Podner's paw. He yelled and hopped about holding the injured foot.

"Now see what you made me do," Polly scowled at Courtleigh.

"Children, please!" Jocelyn cried. He was carrying a tray laden with cans of coke, packets of chili flavoured crisps and ginger chip cookies. It was not Gran's breakfast, but it would do. They sat cross legged on purple cushions and ate. Jocelyn nibbled a few crisps, then took a sip from a bottle of clear liquid, that Polly thought was petrol and Courtleigh knew was vodka. "Do tell what brought you to my door," he said.

"We were running away from the Scooper," Polly began.

"Terrible thing. So noisy, so uncouth, but at least it does try to keep the place clean. The stuff that finds its way down here!"

Podner pulled a face. "Not you," Polly whispered in his ear.

"People are such dirty creatures, but at least I've found a use for some of their detritus." There was a pause as Jocelyn looked expectantly at them.

"It's very nice," Polly said politely.

"Cool," Courtleigh added.

"So glad you like it. I do my best to keep the place beautiful, but it is so hard. The people that come down here! They are the worst of both worlds. No one wants them, so they slink down into The Edges and make my life a misery. Most of them are mad, you know, which is a good thing too, because if they ever catch a glimpse of something they shouldn't, no one believes them."

"I told them. It's not a good place for 'umans," Podner growled.

"I should say not," Jocelyn agreed.

"I think we ought to go." Courtleigh was beginning to feel distinctly unwelcome.

"Oh no. I didn't mean you. You're not trash. At least I don't think you are and it's simply ages since I had anyone to talk to."

"But we've got to get back," Polly said.

Jocelyn put his hand on her arm. She tried to pull away but his grip was firm.

"Just stay for a little bit longer," he coaxed.

Podner shook his head and growled softly from the back of his throat. Jocelyn rolled his head round his neck. "I would so like to tell you a story," he murmured, fluttering his lashes.

Courtleigh moved towards the door. "We really don't have time, thank you," he said politely.

"I suppose not, but I do want to know about dragons," Polly said.

"Oh my dear, of course." Jocelyn lifted his hand and gestured towards the cushion. "Do sit and I'll tell all."

Polly settled herself on the cushion. Courtleigh pulled a face, but he came back and reluctantly sat down beside her. Podner gulped, as if he wanted to say something, but didn't dare. Jocelyn stood with one hand on his hip, the other he raised, pointing one finger upwards as he spoke. "I am, as you can see, a shape changer. All the old families have some powers, but only the best can change their shapes and only the most noble of them are of the dragon line."

"You mean every one can do it?" Polly was puzzled.

"No, no, not at all. Haven't you heard a word I said? It's only the old families."

"Aren't all families old?" Polly asked. Jocelyn raised his eyes to the roof and heaved an elaborate sigh.

"It's to do with magic. Gran told me. Way back," Courtleigh said quickly.

Jocelyn gave him a pained smile. "So your Gran is one of the Hidden Ones is she?"

"Dunno."

"Oh she must be. That's the only explanation. From an inferior family of course."

"There's nothing wrong with my Gran," Courtleigh bristled.

"Of course not. I'm sure she's a very good woman. It's just that she's not from the top drawer."

"I still don't understand. Why's Courtleigh's Gran hidden and what have drawers got to do with it?" Polly said.

"Oh dear, I sense we have to go back to the very beginning."

"It might help," Polly agreed.

"Little girl, be quiet and listen. You must know that at the very beginning of time, when the world was new, there were, in our universe, two different races, humans and angels. Most of the angels stayed in their own sphere, but some came down to earth, where they fell in love with and married humans. That is where we come from. We are the old ones and we all have some sort of power, though naturally some are more special than others.

At first we had our own kingdoms. Wonderful places with names like Atlantis and Tir-an-Og, they were rich and magical lands, where everyone lived in peace and happiness. But of course that could not last. There were wars, terrible, terrible wars and after them came ruin and decay. Our people began to leave and to use their powers among the tribes of men.

For centuries we were respected and honoured. Some of us were kings and priests, others great scientists and artists. Occasionally our power got out of hand. The old quarrels surfaced and there were disasters, like that fire that destroyed much of London and then not so long ago, on a much more minor level, the explosion at the firework factory. But mostly we kept ourselves to ourselves, especially the more ordinary families, who lived quietly and did a little healing magic now and again." He stopped and looked pointedly at Courtleigh.

"You would have thought mankind would have been grateful. You would have thought we'd have been thanked and cherished, but oh no, human beings are a jealous, cold hearted lot and very soon they began to call us evil. They accused us of dabbling in the Black Arts, they burned and stoned us and, oh," Jocelyn gave a great sigh and clutching his chest he began to wheeze. "It upsets me so."

His hand reached out for his inhaler and as it did so the skin thickened and the fingers curved into a claw. His face grew thinner, his body broader. Half man and half dragon, he lay back on his cushion and took deep shuddering breaths.

"What's happening to him?" Polly cried.

"'E can't control 'imself. That's what. Can't 'old onto 'is shape. That's why 'e 'as to live down 'ere, for all 'e boasts about 'is posh family. Now come on, let's get out of 'ere. You can't trust these shape changers. Slippery things they are, so never tell them nothing, cos they'll use it against you."

"Not Jocelyn," Polly protested.

"Specially 'im," Podner said darkly. "Believe me I know. I'm the best."

Courtleigh took hold of Polly's hand and pulled her to her feet. Followed by Podner they crept towards the door.

As it shut behind them, Polly thought she caught a glimpse of a young man, with white blonde hair talking quickly into his mobile. "Yes," he was saying, "yes Sir, I've definitely got something that will interest you." But when she looked again, all she saw was a pale dragon lounging on a purple cushion.

They hurried along the tunnels. Podner scurrying behind them, snapping at their ankles when they slowed down, keeping them going, until at last they could run no longer.

"That was something," Courtleigh gasped.

"A dragon! I thought they only happened in stories," Polly panted.

46

"And where do you think the stories come from?" Podner said, his furry chest rising and falling, as he struggled to catch his breath.

"People make them up."

"But they got to make them up from something."

"I suppose so. So dragons really exist, but they're shape changers. What are the Hidden Ones then?"

"Them what 'ave to keep their powers secret. That is to say, most of 'em nowadays. Now come on. Nor more questions 'til we 'ave you safe."

There might be lots of people like that, that no one knows about, Polly thought as she stumbled on trying to keep up with Courtleigh and out of reach of Podner's snapping teeth. Her legs ached and she was getting very tired, when she heard the first faint warning rumble.

"The Scooper's back. It's come to get us," Podner gasped. Polly took one arm, Courtleigh the other and they whisked Podner into the air, his feet whirling like windmills as they ran. Somewhere at the furthest end of the tunnel there was a faint line of daylight. The ground sloped upwards, the gap was getting wider, they could hear the noise of traffic. They were almost there, when Courtleigh's foot hit a rock. He stumbled, put out his hand to save himself and let go of Podner. Polly held on. She tried to swing him up onto her back, but there was a slurp, his paw slid out of her grasp, then something black was flapping at her face. She yelled and hit out with her fists, but hands closed round her arms, she was lifted off her feet and carried swiftly away.

CHAPTER SEVEN

Courtleigh sat up slowly. There was earth in his mouth and his nose and a terrible banging noise in his head. He tried to stand, but his legs shook so much that he staggered back against the wall. The last thing he remembered was running with Polly and Podner, then the shooting pain in his toe, as it hit that sharp stone.

In front of him he could see daylight, behind him a thick black darkness, out of which came a flapping, shuffling noise and a smell like used cat litter. Courtleigh did not stop to think, he gathered his strength and hobbled towards the light.

The tunnel opened at the back of an old house. The windows were boarded up and the garden was wild with brambles and long grass. He sank down on a broken step and put his head in his hands. He felt sick and dizzy and hurt. They could have waited. Polly was just in front of him when he'd tripped. He remembered her grabbing Podner and running. There was only one way she could have gone and since she was not here she must have decided to go off without him. He didn't care. Not really. It just went to prove what he'd always known, that you couldn't trust anyone except Gran.

Miserably, he rubbed his sore feet. What he needed was some trainers and if he was right about where he had come out, he was at the back of the High Street, where there were plenty of places to get a pair.

The Shoe Box was crammed with display racks, which covered the walls and took up almost all the space in the middle of the shop, so that it was very easy to slip something into a pocket without being seen. He was reaching for a pair of green canvas boots, when a plump lady with grey hair bore down on him.

"Can I help you dear?" she said.

"Thank you, no Mam," he replied politely, remembering that Gran had always told him that when in trouble he was to mind his manners. The assistant smiled and moved away, but Courtleigh knew that she would keep an eye on him until he left. Wishing he was near the big ShoeMart at the edge of town, he began to back out of the shop.

The man waiting at the corner saw him go. His eyes glowed under the brim of his hat and his thin lips twisted into a smile. He pulled the keys from the pocket of his black rain coat and walked silently towards a dark van with blacked out windows.

Courtleigh wove his way through the crowd. Twice someone stood on his toes and by the time he got to the part of town, where Gran lived he was limping badly. The street of small terrace houses was lit by a single old fashioned street lamp. The windows of Gran's house glowed warmly behind red curtains and as soon as his hand touched the gate, the door opened and there she was, a tiny brown skinned lady wrapped in a large shawl.

"What kept you? I saw you were coming this morning, but you've taken so long about it, I was getting worried," she said, as she reached up to give him a quick peck on the cheek.

"There was a bit of trouble, Gran. But…" Courtleigh began eagerly. He was going to tell her that he could do magic too, that he had opened the way into The Edges and saved them from the fire, but before he could start, Gran put her fingers to her lips.

"There's something out here I don't like," she said urgently. She glanced up and down the road, but the black van had parked well out of the range of the street lamp. Gran lifted her face and sniffed the air. "Brimstone," she frowned. "Whatever it is and wherever it's coming from, standing here won't help. Come on in and let me see to those feet."

He followed her down the hall and into the kitchen, where a bowl of water stood waiting in front of the range.

"Stick your feet in that and they'll be as right as rain in no time." Courtleigh sat down and gingerly lowered his feet into the steaming water.

"It doesn't hurt," he said in surprise.

"Of course not. It's meant to heal you, not to hurt you," Gran clicked her tongue impatiently. She took the teapot off the stove and poured two mugs of tea, which she laced with condensed milk tipped straight from the tin. Courtleigh took a sip and leaning back in his chair, let the warm sweetness flow through him.

He loved Gran's house, especially this room with the herbs hanging in bunches from the ceiling, the rag rug on the tiled floor, the blue and white china on the dresser, the two overstuffed armchairs either side of the range and the round table with its velvety cloth, on which stood Gran's crystal ball. He never had to let her know when he was coming home, one glance in the crystal and she knew.

"Feeling better?" Gran asked. He took his feet out of the basin and looked at them. The skin had healed and hardened and the bruises were gone. "There's a new pair of trainers upstairs in your room. I don't know if I got the right ones, but that girl in ShoeMart is too sharp for her own good. I tried the old pendulum trick, but it didn't work. She wouldn't keep her eyes on it long enough to go under. I had to do an invisibility spell in the end. Must be slipping."

Gran shook her head. She never paid money for anything if she could help it, but she always left something in return. A love potion, a cure for acne, good grades in school. No one had ever caught her. It was Courtleigh who was unlucky. Or perhaps she hadn't taught him well enough.

She sighed. It was very difficult to know what to do for the best. He had a father, from one of the old families and a human mother, who was pretty enough, but hadn't a grain of sense in her head. He should have some power of his own, but she had never been able to find it. Why couldn't he run off somewhere one day and find his proper place in the scheme of things? His father had done that. As soon as he was old enough, he'd gone. She'd never seen or heard from him again, not even when his wife and baby turned up. Then the firework factory had exploded and she had been left with Courtleigh.

Ever since he was little, she had wondered what the future held for her only grandson. She had looked into the crystal, but could make no sense of what she had seen.

"They're great. Just the right ones. Thanks Gran," Courtleigh clattered down the stairs and kissed his tiny, little grandmother on the top of her head. "You always get me the best."

Gran smiled, flashing her gold tooth. "That's because you're my best boy. Now we've fixed your feet, you need to eat, so clear the table."

Taking a cloth from the drawer, Courtleigh wrapped up the crystal and carried it over to the dresser. He was very careful not to look inside. Once, when he was little, Gran had sat him on her lap and told him to look deep into the crystal ball. The whirling whiteness had made him ill for days. Fortune telling was not his calling Gran had said, though what was, she really didn't know. Sometimes the worry of what would happen to him disturbed her so much, that all her magic flew about the house in a thousand different strands and she had to be very careful not to open the door to anyone, in case they were accidentally turned into a toad.

Gran fried up bacon, ackees and tomatoes and slid them onto a plate with a generous helping of rice and peas. She sat and watched, until he had eaten every scrap and wiped the plate clean with the rest of the Johnny cakes. "They're still not feeding you properly then?" she said.

Courtleigh shrugged. "It's all right," he said, not wanting to upset her.

Gran frowned. "It's not," she said shortly. "It's all wrong. I know how they treat you. I know you're not happy."

Courtleigh took a deep breath. "Then why do I have to stay? Why can't I be here with you?"

"Because, maybe, it's for the best. Maybe, it's your only chance to be with a family. A real family."

"You're my family," Courtleigh said stubbornly.

"I know. But I'm not like other people. Perhaps I'm no good for you. I don't seem to be able to teach you anything."

Courtleigh opened his mouth. He was going to tell her what he had done, how he wasn't as hopeless as she thought he was, but Gran held up her hand and said firmly,

"Don't interrupt. I know that you've tried and tried. And believe me, not being able to do magic is nothing to be ashamed of. It can happen in the best families. But since you can't, then maybe your only chance is to go out into the world and be like the rest of them and for that you have to learn things that I can't teach you."

"But Gran," Courtleigh thought he was going to burst with impatience. "I've gotta tell you how…"

The room went cold. A deep, dark, cold that chilled the bones and froze the blood. Gran gasped. She grabbed the arms of her chair, her eyes rolled in her head, her whole body jerked, then became still.

There was a terrified miaow. The cat flap clicked and a black cat tore into the room and hid, quivering under Gran's chair. Her eyelids flickered. "There's something evil coming," she whispered.

There was a knock on the door. The cat yowled. The bolts on the front door slid open. Footsteps echoed in the hall. Courtleigh watched the handle on the kitchen door turn, but he could not move.

The man who entered was pale as death, his eyes burning pits in his white face.

"Mrs Jones, I've come for your grandson," said Mr Scythe.

CHAPTER EIGHT

"Put me down," Polly wriggled and kicked, but the things holding her tightened their grip and kept on running. She could see the daylight disappearing and the darkness growing deeper. Soon the only light was from saucers of burning grease set in holes in the wall. Polly gritted her teeth and tried to block out the smell of rancid fat and rotting garbage. "If you don't let me go, I'll be sick."

Her captors lurched to a halt and she slid to the ground, her feet sinking ankle deep into rubbish. She wiped her hands down her jeans and tried to move away, but the creatures pressed closer, almost overpowering her with their stink. Some were adults and some were children and they all looked as if they had been frozen half way through a change from one sort of being to another. Some had human faces, others the bodies of beasts. Their clothes were tattered and filthy and most had wrapped dark cloaks around their shoulders or over their heads, as if to hide what they could of their misshapen bodies.

"What a pretty girl," growled a dog headed man.

"So sweet and fresh," hissed a girl with the body of a serpent and the legs and tail of a dragon. She ran her claws up Polly's arm and pinched her cheeks. A boy with scaly skin and a ridge of spines down his back, elbowed her away. He closed a damp hand around Polly's wrist. The snake girl lashed her tail. "Get lost Boyd, she's mine."

"Don't think so, Cassie."

As they squared up to each other, Polly twisted free and was backing away, when something floated towards her. Its skin was shiny and transparent like a jelly fish. Its veins were red and blue, its bones black. Only the thin strands of hair straggling from the top of its head was a sign she had once been human.

"She has such warm blood," the creature murmured sadly. "Not cold, not broken, not lost. Can I touch? Can I feel?" What might be fingers moved towards Polly's face. She felt sick at the thought of those slimy tentacles running over her skin. But the creature was so sad, all she wanted was some human contact, how could she step away? Before she had to make a choice, however, the snake girl hissed,

"I got her Lakey," and the jelly like creature slid away.

Polly clutched her lucky charm; she glanced behind her to see which way she could run, but the things were coming at her from every side.

"Why did they let you go?" the dog headed man thrust his face into hers.

"Who? What? What are you talking about?" Polly cried.

"Don't ask," something moaned.

56

"But I want to know what's happening." The creatures growled and ground their teeth. *I can't run, but I can kick,* Polly thought. She was lining up where to start, when a squeaky voice broke through the din.

"Let her be," it said and the crowd parted and she was alone in front of a huge pasty faced woman wearing an enormous turban with a fork and spoon stuck into it.

"I am Mad Magda. These are my people. They do what I tell them," she cackled.

She spun round and her dress billowed round her vast hips and the ends of her turban began to unravel. "Bet you've never seen anything like us before," she boasted.

Polly shook her head. Not even in her worse nightmares had she imagined anything as horrifying and terrible as this. "And now you're never going to see anything else." Mad Madga gave a chuckle and another turn of her strange dance.

"What do you mean, I'm never going to see anything else?" Polly felt something like a fist clench in her stomach.

"Well, now we've seen you, we can't let you go. Who knows where you'd go running to? Who knows who you'd tell?"

"I wouldn't tell anyone."

"But we can't be sure of that, can we? And if you did, they'd be down here to get us. To get the last little bits of us." There was a sigh like wind through trees and the rest of the Night People crept closer. "They think they've got it all, you see. But some us was clever. When the doctor did his experiments, we didn't give everything. So if they ever knew, they'd be back."

"I wouldn't tell. I promise," Polly said as convincingly as she could. Mad Magda ignored her. "Your sort are the worst. You look as if nothing happened to you. You sound as if nothing happened to you. Up there everyone would think you're all right. But we know better. We know you belong down here with the rest of us."

"I don't. I don't belong anywhere," Polly cried.

Magda put a small, white, puffy hand on her arm. "Don't be silly dear. You're here now and here's where you're staying. You'll soon get used to us and our funny little ways."

"Nothing happened to me; no one did any experiments on me. So let me go," Polly insisted.

Mad Magda shook her huge head and another layer of her turban came apart.

"Oh no dear. If they didn't take you to the lab and they didn't do their tests on you, that means you've never had any powers. You're not one of us, so we can't let you go back up, in case you tell anyone what you've seen."

Polly looked round at the Night People. "They wouldn't believe me."

"They might. And you see we can't risk it." Mad Magda cocked her enormous head. A pair of scissors tinkled to the floor, followed by a chewed ball point pen and a bent spanner.

It wasn't fair. It was too stupid. How could anyone think she, Polly Miller, was like these creatures. Polly's anger bubbled and boiled. It scorched her throat and as she breathed out, flames leapt from the lamp on the wall and caught the end of Madga's turban. She screamed and the Night People flapped around her, fanning the flames, as they tried desperately to put them out. Polly seized her chance and ran.

Behind her she heard the shrieks and howls of the Night People. In front of her she saw a line of spluttering grease lights and beyond them darkness. She ran until her legs began to wobble and she was in danger of falling over onto her nose. Leaning against the side of the tunnel, she gulped in mouthfuls of dry earthy air. There was no smell of musty rubbish and dead fish. The Night People had not followed her, now all she had to do was to find her way back to the surface and she would be safe.

She looked around, but she could see nothing. She had put her torch in her rucksack at Jocelyn's and she took it out and shone the beam around the walls of the tunnel. *I wish Podner was here, she thought. And Courtleigh. He was just behind me. Then he tripped and the Scooper came. Why did the Night People take me not him? Was it because they thought I was one of them?*

She remembered the stench of their filthy rags and shuddered. She knew she was not some sort of half being, but she also knew she was different from the other kids in the foster homes she had been in, or the ones she had met at school. No one else was followed by a trail of fires everywhere they went. Everyone else had some sort of family. Polly touched her lucky charm and straightened her shoulders. As usual she was on her own and as usual she would make the best of it. Full of determination she hoisted her rucksack onto her back and set off.

She kept her ears strained for the first rumble of the Scooper, but the tunnels were quiet and she was growing tired and hungry. She was also lost. The torch was getting fainter, the darkness was getting deeper and she could see no sign of daylight. Feeling miserable and rather frightened, she clutched her lucky charm.

If only she hadn't lost Podner. She had tried to hold on to him, but the Night People had grabbed her and the suction on the Scooper had been too strong. Polly thought about the sinister white machine. Like any vacuum cleaner the Scooper would have to be emptied when it was full. If Podner had been sucked up whole, then maybe he'd be dumped somewhere. Perhaps, if she could get to the rubbish heap again, she might find him.

She wished she knew more about this mysterious place under the ground. Were the buildings, half hidden in the earth, remains of the old Kingdom? Had the old ones lived down here, or had their world been buried in some sort of disaster? Jocelyn had said there had been wars and fires. He could tell her more and when she had learned everything she wanted to know about dragons and shape changers, he could show her the way to the surface.

She looked round to see if there was something that would tell her where she was and in which direction she should go to get back to the shape changer's den, but this tunnel looked the same as all the others. Perhaps she was never going to get out, perhaps she would be stuck down here for ever. Polly swallowed and wiped her nose on her sleeve. Crying never solved anything. What she had to do was think.

There was a muffled roar and the ground beneath her feet quivered. A square white shape appeared, blocking the tunnel behind her. A white hose slid out of the darkness and wriggled towards her. Polly flattened herself against the wall. She held her breath hoping it would miss her, but the tube coiled itself around her ankle and began to suck at the bottom of her jeans. She gave it a kick, then beat at it with her rucksack, but still it held on. Desperately, she fastened both hands around it and twisted. There was a faint intake of air, as if the thing was gasping for breath, and she was free.

The force of her escape threw her backwards. The wall behind her crumbled and a gap appeared. The Scooper gave a slurp. The hose waved wildly. Polly took a deep breath and making herself as small as she could, she began to squeeze through the hole.

CHAPTER NINE

The station clock said midnight. From a crack in the wall, on platform two, a foot appeared, followed by a leg, then an arm, a shoulder, a head and finally the rest of a small, squarish body. As soon as she was through, Polly scrabbled frantically in her rucksack, pulled out a dirty white towel and stuffed it into the hole. There was a slurp, a gulp and a choking sound. Polly grinned and rubbed her hands on her jeans. That would fix the Scooper. All she had to do now, was to wait until morning and then find her way to the office. Miss Abramawitch wouldn't be very pleased with her, but when she told her about how unfair the Harrises had been to her and Courtleigh, she would understand. Polly's stomach rumbled. She had not eaten since the snack in Jocelyn's lair.

Half way down the platform there was a machine selling chocolate. Polly searched her pockets for some money. Nothing in one, only a dried up piece of chewing gum in the other. Her mouth watered and she bit her lip hard. She would have to go hungry, until she found Miss A. She clenched her fists and her fingers closed round a small, soft hand. Startled, she looked down. A little boy was standing next to her and it was his hand in her pocket. He had big brown eyes and golden hair. He was trailing a piece of dirty grey blanket.

"Do you want some chocolate?" Polly said. The boy nodded. "Got any money?"

The boy shook his head. He turned his eyes to the machine and stared at it hard. The light came on. There was a whirring and a buzzing and the mechanical grab picked up the biggest slab of chocolate, brought it over to the slide and let go. The bar slipped down into the slot.

"Wow." Polly was impressed. She grabbed the chocolate and tore off the wrapper. She broke off two chunks, crammed one into her mouth and gave the other one to the boy. "How did you do that?" The boy did not reply. He held out his hand and Polly divided up the rest of the chocolate. They munched in silence for a while.

"I'm Polly Miller. What's your name?" she said, when she had finished. The boy wiped his mouth on the corner of his blanket. "OK, so you don't want to talk. Thanks for the chocolate, but I'd better be going."

The boy nodded. He took her hand and waited for her to move. "No. Not you. You'd better get home. It's a bit late for you to be out isn't it?" The boy did not move. "Go on. Someone will be worried. They'll call the police and I don't want them to get me cos there'll be all sorts of trouble. So go away."

She tried to pull away, but his fingers tightened round hers. Polly shook her hand, but the boy's grip grew stronger. "I said, get lost." The boy pulled at her fingers. "I'm not coming with you. I can't. So let me go."

The boy smiled. "Let go of me." Polly's voice grew louder. "I don't know who you are, but I'm going and you're not coming with me." The boy shook his head.

Polly bent down so that her face was on a level with his. Big brown eyes looked trustingly into hers. He pointed to a poster on the wall, which showed a boy and a girl walking hand in hand down a path. They looked like brother and sister. "No," Polly said.

The boy nodded vigorously, then tugged at the strap of Polly's rucksack. She tried to jerk it away, but it slid to the ground. The boy pointed again, then bunched his free hand as if he were holding a pencil.

"You want to write something?" He nodded. "If I let you, will you promise to go home?" The boy looked at her, but said nothing. Polly took out her writing pad and a pencil. "Go on take it."

The boy stared hard at the paper. A B appeared followed by an R then an O, then the rest of the letters, that made up the word BROTHER .

"Stop it," Polly screamed. "I don't have a brother. I don't have a family. Everybody knows that." The little boy grinned and moving closer snuggled up to her side.

The man in the dark hat and raincoat slid through the bolted gates. The two children were arguing, which would make it easier, but as he padded down the platform the boy turned and saw him. Scythe stepped into the shadows, but it was too late. The boy snatched up the rucksack and pulled frantically at Polly's hand. Polly grabbed at her bag, tripped over the blanket and sat down hard. The boy's eyes were wide with fear. He tried to pull to her feet, but it was too late. Looming over them, like a great black spider, Scythe looked down at his clip board.

"Polly Miller?" he said. Polly blinked and nodded. "I am Mr Scythe your social worker." He placed his thick, white hand on her shoulder. Polly scowled.

"Miss Abramawitch looks after me. And him," she added quickly. However annoying he was, she didn't want to leave the kid with the sinister Mr Scythe.

"You are no longer under Miss Abramwitch's care." Scythe smiled an oily smile. "Not now that you are going to St. Savlons."

"I'm not." Polly scrambled to her feet. "I haven't done anything wrong."

"I doubt Mr and Mrs Harris would agree."

"It wasn't my fault." Polly glared up at the corpse like face. "I'm not going." She clenched her fists and at the same time, dug her elbow into the boy's side. "Run," she hissed.

The little boy's eyes flickered round the station and for one moment Polly thought he was going to do what she said, then he pressed himself against her and holding his blanket up, stuck his thumb in his mouth.

Scythe bent from the waist, like a snake about to strike.

"Found you," he said, his voice soft with menace. The boy loosened his fingers and the blanket reared up and billowed into Scythe's face. As he fought to free himself, Polly seized her chance and ran. Dragging the boy behind her, she was half way up the platform and getting closer and closer to the exit, when she was struck across the shoulders. As she gasped for breath, Scythe twisted her arm behind her back and marched her out of the station.

A dark van with blacked out windows waited at the kerb. Scythe unlocked the back doors and thrust Polly inside. She fell awkwardly, bumping against another body and as she struggled to sit up, the boy was thrown in on top of her. The doors slammed and the van moved off.

"That hurt," Courtleigh groaned, rubbing his head.

"Well you shouldn't have been in the way," Polly snapped.

"Oh yeah. I was here first."

"So."

"So nothing." They sat smoldering in silence, as the van slid through the sleeping streets. "Where did you go?" Courtleigh said at last.

"I didn't go anywhere. The Night People took me and the Scooper got Podner." The blanket flapped and whisked Polly across the face, as if to remind her. "Oh yeah and this is Sprog. I found him at the station." The boy's hand slid into hers. He nodded as if to show he approved of the name she had given him. Polly took a deep breath. "He says he's my brother."

"Oh yeah," Courtleigh scoffed.

"Yeah," Polly flared. They scowled at each other in the darkness.

The drive lasted a long time, but eventually the van stopped in front of a pair of heavy iron gates. Scythe slid open the window and pressed the intercom button on the gatepost. "I have the children," he announced.

The gates creaked opened and they bumped over a cobbled courtyard. Scythe killed the engine and they climbed reluctantly out of the back of the van. Above them loomed the great black bulk of St. Savlons. Against the dark sky it looked like a prison. The heavy wooden door was studded with iron and the windows were barred. There were towers on each corner and battlements around the roof, where gargoyles kept watch from the parapets.

They huddled together in the cold night air. Sprog buried his head in Polly's side. He was trembling and she put her arm around his shoulders. Her legs were shaking and her stomach felt heavy. She squeezed him tight and tried to pretend she was not afraid. Beside her Courtleigh shuddered.

"It'll be OK," he said, trying to sound confident, but his voice was too high and shaky.

Polly tried to grin, but her lips quivered and wouldn't go in to the right shape. There was a salty, teary taste in the back of her throat. She wished desperately that she'd tried harder in her last foster home, that she had put up with rosebuds all over her room and a foster mother, who was trying to turn her into the sweet little girl she had always wanted.

Scythe went up the steps and pulled the bell rope. Somewhere deep inside the building a bell tolled. There was a long wait, then the door opened.

CHAPTER TEN

In the doorway, almost blocking the light from the hall, stood Mrs Blatch. She was built like a triangle, with a small head and wide hips. She wore a white overall, white shoes and stockings and white rubber gloves like a nurse. Behind her stood her husband, Mr Blatch, a small man with round glasses and a little black mustache. He also wore a white coat.

"Good evening children." Mrs Blatch smiled her small, pink mouth opening to show small, white teeth.

"Bring them in Scythe. Let's see what you've brought us this time," said her husband.

As Courtleigh, Polly and Sprog filed in, Mr Blatch clicked his teeth and muttered,

"You can't be too careful," and sprayed around them with a can of disinfectant.

"It's the germs, my dears. Since we don't know where you've been, we can't take any chances. Not with all these horrible diseases about," Mrs Blatch explained. "There's a new one every day. Only this morning, I was reading about this bug that brings you out in great big black spots."

"Like ladybirds?" Polly said innocently. "Or roses?" Courtleigh bit the inside of his mouth to stop himself from grinning. Mr Blatch tutted and frowned.

"You boys come with me," he said.

"First I need that." Mrs Blatch pointed a gloved finger at Sprog's blanket.

Sprog shook his head and tried to hide behind Polly. "It wants boiling, bleaching and then burning," said Mrs Blatch.

"No," Polly cried. "It's his."

"It's filthy," said Mr Blatch.

"And full of germs," added Mrs Blatch, gleefully. "Give it to me, little boy." She stepped forward and grabbed at Blanket. Sprog did not move. Blanket slid behind his back. Mrs Blatch leaned towards him, balancing on her toes, she stretched out her hand and the whole of her bottom half wobbled. Blanket whisked round the other side. Mrs Blatch swerved to catch it. Blanket gave a wriggle and flew into the air. Mr and Mrs Blatch flung their arms over their heads. "Bring it down this minute. The germs will get everywhere," Mrs Batch cried.

"I don't think it wants to get washed," Polly said.

"Boiled, bleached, burned," Mrs Batch moaned.

"There, there, my dear." Mr Batch put his arm round his wife's shoulders. "We'll catch it later."

"I don't think so," Courtleigh murmured, as Blanket slid itself quietly into Polly's rucksack.

"Come along, boys," Mr Blatch said. Sprog clutched Polly's hand.

"I'll look after it," she whispered. His grip tightened and his face took on a stubborn look. No one was going to make him move. Polly looked at Courtleigh for help. If Sprog did not do as he was told there would be trouble. Things were bad enough. Everyone knew St. Savlons was the place they sent you when nothing else worked. After that it was youth custody.

Courtleigh understood immediately what she wanted him to do. He put his hand on Sprog's shoulder and whispered something in his ear. The little boy looked up at him, his face trembled, his eyes filled, then he gave a great big grin and let go of Polly's hand.

"See you in the morning," Polly's voice echoed gloomily as he and Courtleigh followed Mr Blatch up the stone staircase. They trailed miserably along an empty corridor, until they came to the boys' dormitory where rows of iron beds stood on the bare floorboards. A single light bulb hung in the middle of the room and gigantic shadows leapt over the walls, as they undressed and got into bed. The blankets were hard and prickly, the sheets smelled of bleach and Courtleigh was sure he could hear someone crying, but when he sat up to look, Sprog was curled up fast asleep, breathing gently.

When they had gone, Mrs Blatch turned to Polly. "Now little girl what you need is a bath." The bathroom at St. Savlons was large and echoey. The walls and floors were tiled in white. There were three or four old fashioned baths in the middle room and one was already steaming with hot water. Mrs Blatch poured in a cup full of disinfectant and told Polly to make sure to wash thoroughly and get rid of all the germs. Then she stood and waited. Polly stared and glowered and refused to move until she went away; only then did she slide into the water and out again as quickly as she could. On a chair by the bath there was a clean towel and a nightdress with St. Savlons written on it, which Polly ignored, pulling on an old football shirt instead.

Three of the beds in the girls' dormitory had had curtains drawn around them, the others were empty and one had its covers turned down. Polly put her rucksack where she could see it, Mrs Blatch appeared to have forgotten about Blanket, but you could never be sure with adults, then she climbed into bed. Her lucky charm bumped against her chest and as she lay back against the hard pillow, she saw the grey shape of Blanket slip out of its hiding place and glide silently out of the room.

It's going to find him, Polly thought and grinned. The kid was a nuisance. It was going to be lot harder escaping from St. Savlons with him. He wasn't her brother, he'd made that bit up. Everyone knew she had no family, but she wasn't going to leave him behind. She'd tell Courtleigh in the morning and then they'd make plans. Polly yawned. St. Savlons was the worst place she had ever been, but for the first time in her life she wasn't completely on her own.

CHAPTER ELEVEN

Polly was woken by the sun shining on her face. She opened her eyes, then shut them again quickly. Hanging over the bed rail was a bright purple jumper, a white shirt and a purple and gold tie. This had got to be a bad dream. It was bad enough being at St. Savlons, without having to go Bolterum High, the worst school in the whole world. Polly yawned and stretched and pretended she had just woken up, but it was no good, the dreaded uniform was still there.

The rest of the dormitory was empty. The curtains round the other beds had been drawn back and make up, shoes and underwear were scattered everywhere. There was a smell of perfume and posters and pictures cut out from music magazines had been tacked to the walls. Polly looked at all the girl stuff and wrinkled her nose in disgust.

In the boy's dormitory, Courtleigh saw the familiar uniform and groaned. Things, he thought could not get much worse. In the bed next to his, Sprog slept with his thumb in his mouth, Blanket curled around his hand. At least he would not have to go to Bolterum High, though the junior school in Hunt Street was probably not much better.

As if he knew that Courtleigh was thinking about him, Sprog woke up and gave him a big grin, then he scrambled out of bed and pulled on his clothes. When he was ready, he picked up Blanket, which looked no bigger than a handkerchief this morning and tucked it into the pocket of his trousers.

The dining room had tall pointed windows a vaulted ceiling and a cold stone floor. Polly was already sitting at a white plastic table. She grinned as they came in and waved her spoon at their bowls of cereal. "It tastes of cardboard, but it's all we're allowed."

Sprog dipped his spoon into his bowl and began to eat. Courtleigh sighed and thought longingly of Gran's breakfasts.

When they had finished, Mrs Blatch came in carrying a tray with three glasses of water and three large pills. "Time for your vitamins, my dears," she twittered. "Now pick up your glasses and take your pills. One, two, three."

Courtleigh threw his up into the air, took a sip of water, caught it in his mouth and swallowed. Then he stood up, spread out his hands and took a bow. Polly gulped hers down, followed by lots of water. She did not see Blanket wrap a corner round the remaining pill and whisk it away.

After breakfast, Mrs Blatch made them rinse out their dishes then put them into a dishwasher, which was so clean that it looked as if it had never been used. Then Polly had to wipe the table with an anti-bacterial

74

cloth, while Courtleigh swept up non existent crumbs and emptied them into a pristine dustbin. When she was satisfied that there was not a single germ left, Mrs Blatch said, "Because today is your first day at St. Savlons, Miss Abramawitch is coming to take you to school. In future, you will catch the school bus, which stops at the gates at seven fifteen, precisely. The little boy will go with his sister and you will get off one stop early to take him to Hunt Street. In the afternoon, you have permission to leave school at three fifteen precisely to walk him back. This arrangement will remain for as long as you are with us."

She pursed her lips and peered hard at them. "I do not think that will be for very long. Children like you rarely remain at St. Savlons for any length of time."

Polly felt something cold slide up her back. Courtleigh clenched his fists and thought hard about Gran. Sprog put his thumb in his mouth.

A car bumped over the cobbles. Gears crashed and squealed. A door banged and the bell rang.

"Miss A," Polly said with relief. She waited until Mrs Blatch had gone to open the door before she asked. "Why do you think no one stays here very long?"

"They probably put you in pies and sell you down the chip shop," Courtleigh said gloomily.

"Stop it." Polly clapped her hands over Sprog's ears. "He's too little. You'll upset him."

In the gloom of St. Savlons, Jenny's hair glowed like burnished copper and her dress was bright with gold and orange sunflowers. Because it was cold, she wore a thick embroidered jacket and green leather boots.

"Polly, Courtleigh, I'm sorry to see you here. But I did warn you that, if things went wrong with Mr and Mrs Harris, St. Savlons was the only place left. And things did go wrong. Rather spectacularly so, from what I've been told." Jenny Abramawitch looked hard at Polly. "The whole house burned to the ground."

"Good," Polly muttered. "They deserved it."

"Fortunately, no one was hurt," Jenny Abramawitch said crisply.

"That's because Courtleigh saved us. They were going to leave us to fry. They didn't care. And I don't see how the fire was anything to do with me. I didn't have any matches, so I couldn't have done it. Nor did Courtleigh. And Sprog wasn't even there. So why do we have to be at St. Savlons? It's not fair," Polly cried.

Jenny Abramawitch sighed. "I'm afraid that there's nowhere else that will have you. As for Sprog, Mr Scythe is in charge of him. From now on, he's in charge of all of you. It's only because he was called away on urgent business, that I can take you to school this morning. This will be the last time I'll see you."

"It can't be," Polly cried. "You've always been my social worker." She rubbed her hand fiercely over her eyes to stop herself from crying. Courtleigh stared at the ground and shuffled his feet. He swallowed hard.

76

"I'm sorry," Jenny said. "I had no choice. Someone higher than me decides these things. I only found out when I came to work this morning."

They followed her miserably to the car. The cream coloured cat with purple tipped ears was asleep on the back seat. When Polly and Sprog got in, she lifted an ear, opened an eye, then stretched and settled herself on Polly's lap. Jenny Abramawitch turned the key in the ignition, the car gathered itself together and leapt forward. Lucy dug her claws into Polly's knee and Polly grabbed hold of her fur and held onto her hard. Courtleigh stared out of the window and said nothing, as they lurched and jolted towards Hunt Street.

Hunt Street Junior was surrounded by a high wire fence. Jenny Abramawitch spoke into the entry phone and the caretaker let them through the gates, which he padlocked behind them.

"Stay in the car Courtleigh and don't move," Jenny said. Courtleigh raised an eyebrow as if to say where could he go, then slumped back and glowered through the windscreen. Lucy cat jumped onto the back of the seat and balancing delicately on his shoulder, butted her head against his, until he stretched up and stroked her under the chin. After a while she began to purr and the warm soothing sound made him feel better.

Jenny Abramawitch took Sprog and Polly into the reception class, where forty small children sat round little wooden tables. Some were quietly drawing, others were poking each other with pencils, one boy was crying and a little girl was fast asleep. The teacher was young and harassed. She took Sprog by the hand and led him to a table.

"I'm afraid he doesn't talk much," Jenny Abramawitch said.

The teacher gave a faint smile. "That will make a pleasant change."

Jenny flushed slightly as if preparing to say something difficult. "In fact he doesn't talk at all," she said quickly. The teacher shrugged and Sprog gave her a huge grin. For the first time Polly wondered if perhaps his brain wasn't scrambled. Then she remembered the chocolate machine at the station and thought that if he could do that, then he could not be as dim as he seemed. She was still puzzling over this as she followed Jenny Abramawitch to the car.

"Is everything all right?" Jenny Abramawitch looked at Lucy. The cat licked a paw and began to wash her face. "Then we had better get going, or we'll be late." She put the car into reverse. It leapt back, just avoided smashing into the fence, then jolted forward and made a run at the gate. The caretaker stepped smartly to one side and they juddered down the road.

Although it was almost nine o'clock, the streets round Bolterum High were still full of pupils in purple uniforms. They strolled and chatted and ate burgers and drank out of cans and one or two smoked, staring defiantly at Jenny Abramawitch, as she steered in between the groups that spilled off the pavements and out into the road. When they got to the school gates, Lucy cat gave a little miaow.

"We trust you to go straight in," Jenny Abramawitch said to Courtleigh, as she banged the car into the kerb. "I need you to keep an eye on Polly," she called as he scrambled out.

Courtleigh sighed. He had worked out that if instead of going to class, he went into the PE block, he could get rid of blazer and tie and if he customized his shirt and found himself a pair of dark glasses from somewhere, he could slope off and stay out all day without anyone catching him. He looked back and saw Lucy cat staring at him, as if she knew exactly what he was thinking. Beside her sat Polly looking very small in her new uniform.

"O.K. Will do," he muttered and sticking his hands in his pockets, he walked off towards a group of boys he knew.

When they got to reception, Jenny Abramawitch tapped firmly on the glass partition, which separated the office from the entrance hall and spoke for a long time to one of the secretaries. While Polly was waiting for her to finish, the bell went for the end of assembly and a tide of purple swept down the main corridor. The older pupils looked mean and tough and the younger ones came out of the hall hitting each other and shouting insults. Polly stood back against the wall and watched them. She looked for Courtleigh, who saw her and waved, but she didn't see him.

"Hullo. Are you new?" said a skinny kid with glasses and a jumper that was too tight. "I'm Kevin. I'm Host of the Day and I've got to take you to see Mr Croft to sort out your timetable." He pushed his glasses back up his nose and trotted off down the main corridor. Polly hoisted her rucksack onto her back and was wandering after him, when the double doors swung open and three girls appeared.

One was dark, her skin so black it shimmered. She had dyed her hair a brilliant scarlet, tied her tie round her head and wore a skirt that barely reached the top of her thighs. The middle one had spiked white blonde hair, slightly slanted green eyes and coffee colored skin, while the third was white with dead black hair, cut in a bob. She had drawn thick black lines round her eyes and her tie was around her waist. Shoulder to shoulder they sauntered down the corridor.

"Oh cripes, Shaz, Maz, and Baz," Kevin gulped. His eyes darted from side to side and beads of sweat erupted like pimples on his forehead. "Excuse me. I got to go," he muttered and dived into the boys' toilets.

Polly looked around for somewhere to hide, but it was too late. Shaz, Baz and Maz had seen her. Side by side, moving in step, they strolled towards her. Polly's stomach fluttered. Her legs felt weak, but she did not move. To turn and run would show she was scared. She pressed her lucky charm and prayed that a teacher would appear, but the classroom doors stayed shut and the girls kept coming, swinging their hips and glaring, until they were looming over her.

"You're new," said the girl with the red hair. Polly nodded. Her mouth was too dry to speak.

"That's why you don't know," said the one with the blonde spikes.

"What everyone else knows," the third girl hissed.

"That you don't mess with us," snarled the girl with the scarlet hair.

"Show her why, Shaz," said the blonde. Shaz grinned. Her nails were very long and very sharp and she dug them hard into Polly's arm.

"So now she knows," the dark haired girl grinned evilly. She opened her mouth and chewed loudly. Then she spat. The gob of gum went straight in Polly's face. She could not help herself. She lowered her head and charged. Baz screamed and doubled over. Shaz grabbed at Polly's hair and yanked back her head, but not before Polly had sunk her teeth into her wrist.

"Maz get the little cow," Shaz screamed.

"I'm not a cow," Polly yelled. "I'm Polly Miller and you don't spit at me." The fury inside her bubbled and simmered and exploded. At that moment the fire bell rang and suddenly the corridor was swarming with people. Polly gave her attackers one final kick and dived into the crowd.

It carried her out into the yard, where teachers flapped about trying to get their forms to stand in line, so that they could take the registers. The pupils of Bolterum High, however, had no intention of co-operating. They milled around laughing and shrieking, while from a ground floor window, a thin streak of smoke rose into the sky.

"Silence," the headmaster screamed into his megaphone. No one took any notice.

"When I find out who is responsible they will be expelled on the spot," he shouted.

Instantly half a dozen hands shot up.

"Please sir, it was me sir. I done it," shouted a group of Year Sevens.

"Be quiet all of you." The head turned as purple as his pupils' uniform.

From somewhere in the distance came the sound of a fire engine. The whole school booed and yelled, then cheered and clapped as Shaz, Baz and Maz strolled out into the yard. Maz settled herself down on a low wall, Shaz opened a jar of wax and together she and Baz began tweaking the blonde strands into even fiercer spikes.

Not even the fire chief could silence the pupils of Bolterum High. It took until lunch time and a shower of rain before the fire, which had broken out in a lab on the main corridor, was put out and the pupils wandered back inside.

"I don't know how it happened," quavered Mr Goodhew, the chemistry master. "We weren't using the bunsens. I haven't dared to do an experiment in years. 9F were taking notes, just taking notes." He wrung his hands and had to be taken to the office and given a large dose of the brandy, which was kept there for medicinal purposes.

Polly sat in reception and waited for someone to tell her where she should go. At ten past three, she went to the window and told the secretary, very politely, that she had special permission from her social worker to leave early to collect her little brother. Then she slipped her rucksack onto her shoulders and walked out of Bolterum High.

At Hunt Street there were clusters of mums around the gate. Polly wriggled her way to the front just as the bell rang and the children came out into the yard. Sprog was trailing Blanket, which seemed longer and dirtier than it had that morning. When he saw her, he grinned and Blanket lifted its edge in a sort of wave. Polly took his hand. She knew there was no point in asking him about his day, so she talked what had happened at Bolterum High.

"There were these three girls. They tried to scare me, but I didn't let them. They'll try again tomorrow, so I'll have to be ready. Courtleigh could have warned me," she said. "Oh and there was a fire. They had to have the fire brigade."

The cream coloured cat padding behind them, curled her tail into a question mark, as if thinking about what Polly had said. Keeping her distance, she followed, until they reached St. Savlons, when she jumped over the wall and disappeared.

Outside the gate was a notice, which read in faded gold letter. "St. Savlons Care Home." Over it someone had scrawled in red gloss, "St. Savlons Don't Care Home. Give up now." Polly pulled a face and Sprog clutched Blanket as the gates swung open.

"They don't mean it," Polly said, trying to reassure him. "Come on. We've got to go in." Sprog's bottom lip trembled and he shook his head.

"It's no good crying. If you'd done what I said at the station we wouldn't be here now." She yanked at his arm and he stumbled after her through the gates. As they closed silently behind them, Polly shuddered. Once they were inside, there would be no way out, until they caught the school bus in the morning.

The front door was firmly shut. There was no handle only an iron bell pull. They had to make their way round the side of the building and in through a small door at the back. In the kitchen a slim girl with blonde hair and blue eyes stood stirring something on the stove.

"There you are," she smiled. "I've made some hot chocolate and there's a plate of cookies on the table. You must be cold and hungry after that walk. It will be a while until supper, so eat up." The chocolate was hot and creamy with flakes of grated chocolate floating on top. The cookies were warm and gooey. The girl put on a cream leather jacket, then pulled on a lilac knitted hat and a matching pair of gloves.

"See you tomorrow," she said and as she went out, Polly heard the sound of a key turning in the lock.

"They've got us now," she said, licking the chocolate from her fingers. "There's no getting out." Sprog wiped his face on the edge of Blanket and slid off his chair. Polly shook her head in exasperation. "You don't care, do you?" He looked at her with his big brown eyes and she felt like shaking him. If he had let her go, that night at the station, she might have got to Miss Abramawitch, who could have saved them. She turned to rinse out their mugs and Sprog slipped out leaving the door wide open.

The sound of the television wafted down the corridor and echoed round the empty kitchen. It was a cold, lonely noise that made Polly hurry to the common room, where she was sure she would find Courtleigh.

"Why didn't you tell me…?" she began, as she flung open the door. Then stopped and stared in horror.

Sprawled on the settee, filing her nails into sharp points, was Shaz. Lying on the floor flicking through a magazine was Maz, while Baz sat on the chair by the gas fire with Sprog curled up beside her.

"Well look who's here," Shaz drawled.

"It's the new girl," said Maz.

"The one that thinks she's not scared of us," said Baz.

CHAPTER TWELVE

Polly stood at the door of the common room and looked round for help. Courtleigh shrugged his shoulders and gave sheepish grin. Sprog snuggled closer to Baz.

"You're a little darling aren't you," Baz ruffled his hair.

"Traitor," Polly hissed.

Maz slid to her feet. "Leave him alone."

"Don't upset him," Baz said.

"Or we'll do you," Shaz finished.

"But he's supposed to be *my* brother," Polly said bitterly.

"He's the cutest little one we've had for ages," Baz said. "So he won't be here for long."

"What do you mean?"

"She wants to know what we mean." Shaz uncurled herself from the sofa. She joined Maz and they closed in on Polly. "Don't you know that no one stays long at St. Savlons? No one that's sweet, or pretty or cute."

"They all get adopted," Maz said. "Except us. We're too old and too hard."

"That's right. Nobody wants us." Shaz flicked her long red nails in Polly's face. "And no one will want you either."

"You're too fat and too ugly and too stupid," said Maz.

"No she's not." Courtleigh sprung up from his chair. "Come on Polly, we're getting out of here."

"They've locked all the doors and windows. You haven't got a hope," Shaz yelled after them.

"Why didn't you tell me?" Polly said, as the mocking laughter followed them down the corridor.

"Dunno. Thought you'd find out soon enough. They're not that bad."

"Not that bad! They tried to beat me up this morning."

"They do that to all the new kids," Courtleigh said, as if it did not matter.

"Yeah, but the new kids don't have to live with them."

"You stood up to them."

"That will make them hate me more," Polly said despondently.

"It won't," Courtleigh tried to comfort her.

"It will. It's bad enough being here, without Baz, Shaz and Maz." Polly pulled a face and looked down the tall, thin corridor. Lit by a single light, it was full of shadows and the smell of old cooking and bleach. "It's horrible here. Can't we run away?"

"They'll only catch us again," Courtleigh said. Polly looked so miserable that he wished he could do something to make her feel better, or at least give her some reason for wanting to stay. He crossed his fingers behind his back and prepared to lie. After all what did it really matter if it was true or not, Polly wanted to believe it and perhaps it would change her mind about running away. "What about Sprog? He's your brother, we can't leave him here."

"Oh no?" Polly said bitterly. "He likes Baz better than me, so he can be her brother. I don't care. I'm going to find a way out."

"Oh man," Courtleigh sighed. He pushed his baseball cap to the back of his head and loped after her.

Polly charged past the empty, echoing rooms on the ground floor and galloped up the stone staircase that led up to the dormitories. On one side were three long rooms that made up the boys' quarters, on the other were the same number for the girls. All the windows were barred and in each room there were twenty beds, all neatly made. She looked down the rows and shivered. Once over a hundred orphans had lived here, now there were only six of them. What had happened to all the others and why did the rooms feel as if they were still waiting?

"It's spooky," she said.

"It's weird man," Courtleigh agreed. They looked at each other.

"We've got to get out of here," Polly said.

"Yeah, but how? The doors are all locked and they've got bars on all the windows."

"You got us out of the Harrises," Polly pointed out.

OK. I did, but there was an open window for a start and a drain pipe to slide down."

"Maybe if we could get up into one of the turrets, we could find one." Polly refused to give up.

"And then what? Fly?"

"No. You can do what you did before."

Courtleigh thrust his hands into his trouser pockets and scowled. He had no idea how he had opened the way down into The Edges and he did not know whether he could do it again. But he did not want to stay at St. Savlons with its sinister, empty rooms and Shaz, Baz and Maz and the Blatches with their disinfectant sprays and healthy food. "OK. I'll give it a go, but we need a window. There might be some at the top without bars."

They found a staircase and went up to the next floor. Along this corridor all the doors were locked. They were painted a drab brown except for one which was bright blue and looked like an ordinary front door.

"I bet that's where the Blatches live," Courtleigh said. "I bet they don't have iron beds and bathrooms with no locks on the doors."

"It's probably all covered in plastic and stinks of that spray," said Polly. "I had a foster mother who did that once. She was so scared I'd get her new sofa dirty, she never took its wrapper off. And she never let me sit on any of the soft chairs. I left there after the chip pan caught fire." She grinned. "It made the kitchen walls all black."

At the end of the Blatches' corridor, narrow wooden stairs led up to the attics. It was very dark and they went slowly, feeling their way until they got to the top, where Courtleigh ran his hand along the wall and found the light switch. A light bulb hung from the ceiling and in the dim light strange shapes danced across the walls. Polly's hair lifted from the back of her neck.

"Stop it," she swung round at Courtleigh.

"I didn't do anything," he protested.

"You pulled my hair."

"I did not," he said indignantly.

Above them the skylight rattled. A gust of air spiraled downwards, catching their breath and wafting it up out of the broken window. "See, I told you. I knew we'd find a way out," Polly cried triumphantly.

"OK, OK. Give me a minute." Courtleigh was growing more and more nervous. What if he couldn't find the way? Perhaps the last time he had just been lucky and Gran was right and he didn't have any real power. He stared up at the window and pretended he was trying to work out a way to get up to it. "It's too high," he said at last.

"It isn't. You can do it. I know you can." Polly was dancing with impatience.

"Oh yeah?" he snarled.

"Yes," Polly cried, beating her fists against her side. "Go on Courtleigh, please."

He couldn't deny her. He had to try. Maybe she was right. Maybe he could get them out. "OK," he said reluctantly. He took her hand. He closed his eyes. He thought as hard as he could about leaping into the air and up through the open skylight. "Jump," he said.

They jumped. They felt the cold night breeze on their faces and the wind in their hair, then their feet hit bare wooden floorboards. They opened their eyes and saw they were still in the attic of St. Savlons.

"Nothing happened," Polly cried.

"Told you," Courtleigh muttered.

"You didn't try. You don't want to get out of here. You never did. I hate you Courtleigh Jones," Polly yelled and stormed away.

Courtleigh's shoulders slumped. It wasn't his fault. What was it Gran had said? You only went into The Edges in an emergency. So being in St. Savlons wasn't an emergency. It was just something they would have to cope with, until things got better. If they ever did. Miserably, he put his hands in his pockets and sloped after Polly.

CHAPTER THIRTEEN

Polly clattered down the stairs. She was so angry, she did not see Mrs Blatch standing in the entrance hall. She was smoothing down her overall and looking anxiously towards the door. Beside her, Mr Blatch was poised with his spray can. He was about to press the button, when his wife noticed Polly.

"Where have you been?" she demanded.

"Nowhere," Polly said.

"Good. In that case you can get yourself straight back to the others and you," Mrs Blatch waved at Courtleigh, as he tried to sneak past them without being seen. "We have some very important visitors coming here tonight. And if you speak nice and politely to Lady Serena, who knows you might just be the luckiest children and find wonderful new homes. So off to the common room with you and don't move from there until you're told."

In the common room the television was turned up as loud as it would go. Shaz, Baz and Maz were draped over the chairs and sofas, but there was no sign of Sprog.

"Not found the way out yet?" drawled Baz .

"Come to see if anyone wants to take you home," Maz mocked.

Polly scowled. She found a space as far from everyone as she could and stared blankly at the television. On the opposite side of the room, Courtleigh sat with his back against the wall, refusing to look at her. He had tried his best to get them out of St. Savlons. It wasn't his fault it hadn't worked. Why wouldn't she understand?

Mr Blatch puttered in like a little steam engine. He switched off the television and aimed his spray. Shaz began to cough. Then Maz joined in, holding her side and making terrible choking noises. Frowning, Mr Blatch looked at his can, then at the girls and tried to make up his mind, whether spraying them would make things better or worse.

"You'll poison us. We'll be lying here in a heap and then what will your important visitors say then?" said Baz.

Reluctantly, Mr Blatch lowered his disinfectant. "Get up, get up," he sputtered. "They'll be here in a minute. Can't you at least show them you've got some manners?" Shaz slid a glance around the room and shook her head. "Please," begged Mr Blatch. No one moved.

The door opened. Mr Blatch gulped, his throat moved up and down and he began to nod furiously. His face turned very red.

"Good evening my lady," he stuttered.

Lady Serena swept in on a wave of expensive perfume. She wore white trousers, white boots and a long white coat that skimmed the ground. Her hair was dark, her skin white, her eyes green as the emerald she wore on her finger.

"We're looking for a child," her voice was low and soft, but her eyes were cold.

"Take your pick," Shaz said rudely.

Lady Serena ignored her. "I was told you had a little boy here; a blonde little boy. Rather like my dear Dr Lindstrom." She turned to the man, who had come in behind her. He was tall and fair with icy blue eyes behind lightly tinted glasses. She put one hand on his arm and smiled up at him.

"We've got just the child you want. Mr Scythe brought him in yesterday," Mrs Blatch said. Eagerly she looked around the room. Then her forehead wrinkled and she put a hand on her chest. "Where is he girls? He was here a minute ago."

"Dunno," Maz said. Shaz shrugged, Baz shook her head.

"I tell you he was here. I saw him," Mrs Blatch's voice rose. No one said anything.

Lady Serena frowned. "Mrs Blatch, this is not like you. We can usually rely on you to find us exactly the sort of child we are looking for. That is why our donations to your home are so generous." She glanced pointedly at the multi entertainment system. "I can see you are making good use of our money," she said dryly.

"Oh yes, yes." Mrs Blatch trembled, drops of sweat fell from her forehead as she cried, "We'll find him. It won't take long, he's only small, he can't have gone far. Herbert go and look in the boy's dormitory. Girls, and you boy, go and search. Go on find him. Don't sit there. Hurry, hurry." She flapped her hands at them as if shooing flies.

Very, very slowly, Baz, Shaz and Maz got to their feet. Baz stretched, Maz yawned and Shaz smoothed down imaginary creases in her skintight jeans. They strolled towards the door, muttering and complaining.

"And you and you," Mrs Blatch waved at Polly and Courtleigh.

The three girls were waiting for them in the entrance hall.

"You go upstairs. We'll do this floor," Maz said .

"Don't try too hard," Shaz added, sounding suddenly very serious.

"Cos, maybe," Baz said. "He doesn't need to be found." She linked arms with her friends and they strolled casually down the corridor.

"What does she mean?" Polly asked Courtleigh.

"Don't know." He sat down on the stairs and stretched out his legs. Polly joined him.

"Aren't we going to look then?" she said.

"In a bit."

They sat for a while longer. Long enough for a small boy to hide himself thoroughly, then they went upstairs and looked in some cupboards and under one or two beds. Finally, Courtleigh said, "We tried."

Polly opened her eyes wide and said in an innocent voice, "But we couldn't find him."

In the common room, Shaz, Baz and Maz sat on the sofa glaring at the visitors, who were talking quietly to each other.

"Where is he?" Mrs Blatch bounced up and down on her toes.

"I'm sorry my dear. I can't seem to find him anywhere," Mr Blatch said fearfully.

His wife grabbed his arm. "Herbert it's not possible. It's just not possible. We've never lost a child from St. Savlons. Never."

"I'm sure you haven't. No doubt he will turn up soon," Lady Serena said smoothly.

"If you wait, it's almost supper time. He'll be hungry and he'll come out, you'll see." Mrs Blatch was getting more and more agitated. Dr Lindstrom looked at her coldly.

"That won't be necessary. We can always come back another time. When you have him secure. Come my dear" he took Lady Serena's arm and began to lead her towards the door.

"All I wanted was a little blonde boy like you," she said softly. She lifted her hand to her face as if wiping away the tears, but her eyes were quite dry.

"There will be another one. They come in all the time. You don't want this one. He's not all there. He doesn't even talk," Mrs Blatch cried desperately.

The man and woman glanced at each other. He raised an eyebrow and she nodded briefly.

"He's stupid," Mrs Blatch said, bluntly.

"No, he's…" As Polly rushed in to defend her brother, the three girls rose from the sofa.

"Excuse her, she's thick," Shaz swaggered towards Lady Serena, hiding Polly from view, while Maz clapped her hand over her mouth and Baz hissed,

"Shut up. Can't you."

"He's blonde and that is what I want," Lady Serena sighed.

"We'll find him, we'll find him," Mr Blatch repeated urgently, as he hurried after their visitors.

"Come along on children. Come and say goodbye to Lady Serena and Dr Lindstrom. The Bioflex Foundation has done so much for St. Savlons. You must show how grateful we all are." Mrs Blatch hustled them into the entrance hall, where she made them line up on the front steps.

A long dark car slid up. Dr Lindstrom opened the door for Lady Serena.

"Remember, we want the boy," he said. By tomorrow. Otherwise he'll lose the chance of a life time."

Mr and Mrs Blatch nodded furiously.

As the car drew away. Courtleigh dug Polly in the ribs.

"Look at the driver," he whispered. "It's Scythe."

CHAPTER FOURTEEN

Mrs Blatch was furious. Didn't they know how lucky they were to be at St. Savlons, because nowhere else would have them? They were stupid, ungrateful, children, who did not realize how good Lady Serena was. They had her to thank for the television and those things they played their music on. If it wasn't for her, there would be no healthy food, or hot water and they would all get germs and die.

When she had finished, Shaz gave an enormous yawn and said that if they didn't have supper soon, they would all die of starvation anyway. Mrs Blatch began to quake; she rocked on her feet, she shuddered and bounced. Her whole body trembling with rage, she raised her arm.

"She's going to hit you," Maz said loudly.

"No, no," Mrs Blatch spluttered. "How can you say that? You know we don't have corporal punishment at St. Savlons."

"Only because it's too messy and might cause germs," Shaz said cheekily, as she led the way to the dining room. Sitting at one of the tables, holding onto Blanket was Sprog. "Look who's here," she cried.

Maz ran over and gave him a hug. Baz ruffled his hair. Courtleigh slapped him lightly on the back.

"Hi," Polly said coldly. He was supposed to be her brother and she couldn't get near him for all the fuss. The others were all over him and she was left out in the cold.

Shaz gave Sprog's ear a friendly tweak. "I wonder where you've been. We looked ever so hard, but we couldn't find you, could we guys?" She glanced at them all, including Polly, and winked. Courtleigh grinned at her and at once Polly felt better. He lifted his hand and they slapped palms. Sprog smiled delightedly at everyone, then tucked Blanket under his chin and began to eat.

The next day they all traveled to school together. When the Sunny Day Tours bus drew up at the gates, it was already full to bursting with kids in purple uniforms. Polly took hold of Sprog's hand and prepared to fight her way through the crush, but as Shaz, Baz and Maz stepped aboard, the bodies melted away. Kids flattened themselves against the sides, arms and legs hung out of windows, smaller children were thrown on the luggage rack and suddenly there were seats for all of them, even Sprog, who sat calmly holding Blanket and looking out of the window. When they came to his stop Shaz let out a piercing whistle, the driver stood on the brakes and everyone stood aside to let Sprog and Polly get off.

Miss Abramawitch stared at the huge pile of papers on her desk. There were even more heaped up on the floor and on the window sill.

She sighed, as she picked up the first folder and began to read. Something tugging at the back of her mind was making her feel uneasy. At first, she could not think what it was, then she remembered that it was something to do with St. Savlons. Something that made her wish that Courtleigh and Polly were still under her care.

She pushed back her chair and made her way carefully to the filing cabinet. She unlocked the drawer and searched until she found the files. Cassie Saunders, Boyd James and Coralie Brown. All three had been her cases, until they had been sent to St.Savlons. Then what had happened to them? Jenny scanned their notes. At the bottom of the final page, stamped in blood red ink was the word, "Adopted" followed by the name and address of the new parents.

She looked across to the cat, who was asleep on a chair in the corner of the office.

"If it all worked out so well, why don't I feel happy about it? You know Lucy, when I get a minute, I'll check up on those kids." The cat's whiskers twitched, she opened one eye and looked at Jenny. "I know. It ought to be OK, but it isn't. I'm glad you are there to keep an eye on them. I only wish I'd thought of it with the others."

The phone rang. The cat's fur ruffled and she gave a low growl.

"Scythe here." As his voice oozed over the line, Jenny's skin prickled. "I think you should know that there is a problem with one of your children at Springfield School. They need you straight away."

Jenny looked at Lucy and made a face. Springfield was miles away. At this time of day the traffic would be terrible, but if they left immediately, they should get back in time for Lucy to see Sprog and Polly safely back from Hunt Street. She pushed her papers to one side, shook out her skirts and opened her patchwork bag, for the cat to step inside.

Two minutes later, the little red car was juddering and shaking its way out of the car park. Half way there Jenny turned a corner too wildly, hit the kerb and the tire, which had been bleeding air since they set out, gave a final oooff and the car settled gratefully on the tarmac.

At three thirty Polly left Bolterum High feeling pretty pleased with her day. Because everyone knew how she had stood up to Shaz, Baz and Maz, no one had bullied her and she had spent her lunch time with Courtleigh. Eager to tell Sprog all about it, she hurried along, her rucksack bumping against her back, her lucky charm bouncing under her shirt.

As she turned the corner into Hunt Street, the cream coloured cat jumped up on the wall and hastily smoothed her rumpled fur. She had only just made it in time. Another few minutes and she would have missed Polly altogether.

The bell rang and the caretaker opened the gates. Polly looked round the yard, but there was no Sprog. Mums came and went with their children, then there was another bell and the juniors surged through the doors. Shouting, yelling, kicking footballs and swinging bags, they spilled out onto the pavement and Polly searched anxiously, until gradually their noise echoed away and the last child had disappeared down the street.

"They've all gone you know," said the caretaker. "You'd better get off home too, before I lock up."

"I'm waiting for my brother."

"Which class is he in?"

"Year One."

The man shook his head. "They've all gone. The cleaners are in there now."

"He can't have. He has to walk home with me," Polly protested.

"I told you. He's not here. Hey, where do you think you're going? You can't go in there. There's only teachers allowed in there."

The caretaker waved his broom, but Polly dodged past him and dashed in through an open door. She ran down the corridor and burst into Sprog's classroom. The teacher looked up from her desk.

"What are you doing here?" she asked tiredly.

"I'm Polly Miller. I've come to get my brother."

"Of course. You came yesterday. You're David's sister."

Polly nodded wondering who had given Sprog this name and whether he liked it. The teacher smiled at her.

"In spite of his problems, he's a sweet little boy, but I'm afraid you're too late."

"I can't be. I watched all the others come out and he wasn't there," Polly was beginning to feel frightened.

"He left at two o'clock. I had a note from your foster mother." The teacher rummaged in a drawer and brought out a piece of blank paper. She looked at it and nodded. "Oh yes. He had a dentist's appointment. I did tell him dentists don't hurt, but it didn't make any difference, he still looked sacred stiff. It was only a check up. I'm sure he must be home by now."

Polly swallowed hard. "This lady that took him. What did she look like?"

The teacher was puzzled. "Like your foster mother. What else did you expect?"

Polly had to think quickly. She screwed up her face and made herself sound as if she was on the brink of bursting into tears. "I don't live with them. They didn't take me. They only wanted a little boy."

The teacher sniffed. "Some people," she muttered under her breath. "Don't worry." She put her arm round Polly's shoulders. "I'm sure you'll find somewhere as good if not better. Money isn't everything."

"You mean the lady was rich?" Polly's heart was beating very fast.

"She had a very nice car and a chauffeur too I think," the teacher said.

"A kind of slimy man with a dark coat?"

"Yes, I suppose he was," the teacher smiled. "Come on, you'd better go home. Things will get better, you know. Remember it's always darkest before dawn."

Polly raced down the corridor and out into the yard, only to find that the gates were locked. She was yelling for someone to let her out, when the caretaker appeared, carrying black plastic bags.

"Hold your horses," he grumbled. "I'm on my way. You're lucky I was emptying the rubbish. Otherwise you'd have had a long wait. I was working right at the other side of the building."

He fumbled in his pocket for his keys and Polly had to bite her lip to stop herself from screaming at him to hurry up. At last the key was in the lock; the gates were open and she was about to run out, when the caretaker grabbed her.

"Manners," he said crossly.

"Sorry," Polly muttered.

"I don't know. Children nowadays. Spoiled brats the lot of them. Don't just stand there, give me a hand with the rubbish."

He handed Polly a bag and pointed to the row of dustbins on the edge of the pavement. Polly wrinkled her nose and lifted a lid. Like a whirlwind, Blanket flew up into her face and pressed its warm grey wool against her nose and mouth.

"Get off. I can't breathe." Polly fought it off and Blanket quivered and settled around her shoulders, pressing close around her neck, like an animal needing comfort. She dropped the bin lid and ran as fast as she could all the way to St. Savlons, followed by a limping cat with very sore paws.

CHAPTER FIFTEEN

Courtleigh was in the boys' dormitory, when Polly burst in, Blanket billowing out behind her.

"Lady Serena's got Sprog," she cried breathlessly.

Courtleigh felt something cold shudder up his spine. "Not good man."

"They took him straight from school. The teacher said she had a note, but it didn't have anything written on it. It was really weird."

"Inkfade. Gran knows how to do that. After a bit, the ink disappears, but if you've read it once, you think it's still there."

"So the teacher wasn't part of Lady Serena's plan?"

"I dunno. Probably not."

"Where is he then? Where have they taken him?"

"The Blatches will know. If he's your brother, they can't stop you seeing him. Can they?" Courtleigh said doubtfully.

"They would. They're all part of it. They've got to be. They said they'd find him for them. That fat jelly, she'd do anything they want."

Polly's thoughts were whirling in her head. She was sure Sprog was in danger, but who would help them? There was only one person, she had ever been able to trust.

"Miss A will help. We can ask her," she cried. Courtleigh shrugged. "She would," Polly said hotly.

"OK, OK. But how? There's no way we can get to her office and I don't have her number, do you?" Polly shook her head. "Anyway Scythe is in charge of us now," he said gloomily.

"Scythe took them to Hunt St. He was driving the car." Polly's stomach turned over. "He gave them Sprog. Mrs Blatch said no one stays long at St. Savlons and that's why. When someone wants a kid, Scythe hands them over."

Courtleigh shook his head. "No that can't be right."

"It is," Polly said desperately.

"No man. Listen. You can't just give kids away, you've got to do it legally. And anyway not many people want kids our age. Not to adopt that is..." his voice trailed away. He and Polly stared at each other in horror.

"What do they do with them, then?" she said at last.

"I don't know, but we've got to find out."

"How?"

"There's got to be papers. Miss A is always doing forms and things on us, maybe the Blatches have Sprog's papers and stuff in the office," Courtleigh said.

They crept out into the darkened corridor. Courtleigh went first, his cap pulled low over his eyes, sneaking down the stairs as silent as a cat. Polly followed, holding her breath and clutching Blanket, which twisted and turned as it kept watch for the Blatches. Their shadows trailed behind them, like dark clouds in the dim light.

"It's that door on the left," Courtleigh hissed as they reached the ground floor. "There's no one in there. I can't see a light."

Polly clutched at his sleeve. "What if they catch us?"

Courtleigh grinned. "We'll say you've got germs, so we were looking for Mr Blatch. That'll sort them."

He put his hand on the door knob and turned it cautiously. The door creaked open. Polly's heart was beating furiously, Courtleigh's hands were damp. Then Blanket broke free and glided into the empty room.

A brand new computer, its box still on the floor, stood on the desk. There was also a television and a top of the range, multi functional entertainment centre with a pile of films with titles like "Childhood Diseases" and "Operations for Amateurs." Ignoring these Polly marched straight to the filing cabinet. She tugged at a drawer, expecting it to be locked, but it shot out and sent her staggering across the room. She flung her arms in the air, and her feet skittered from side to side in a mad dance, as she tried to keep her balance. In spite of the danger she looked so silly, that Courtleigh had to shove his fist into his mouth to stop himself from laughing.

"It's empty," she gasped, when she finally came to a standstill. "There's nothing in it."

"There's got to be," Courtleigh peered into the drawer.

It was empty, so were all the others. There were no papers for any of them, not for Polly, Courtleigh, Sprog, or Baz, Shaz and Maz.

"That's creepy," Polly said. "Where's my file? It's dead fat. It's got all my stuff in it." She shivered. "It's like we're not here. None of us. Not just Sprog. Courtleigh remember what Mrs Blatch said, nobody stays here long. So where to they go?"

"I dunno. Maybe they get adopted. I know, that's what it is. He's little and cute, so maybe he's gone to a good home," Courtleigh was trying to convince himself.

"Oh yeah! And left Blanket behind."

"I know. It's wrong, but what can we do?"

"I'm not leaving my little brother with that woman. I'm going to find him."

"And how are you going to do that?"

"I dunno, but I'll find a way. You'll see."

Polly whirled round and stormed down the corridor to the common room. "You've got help me get out of here," she cried.

Maz looked up from her magazine. "Why? Where's the fire?"

Baz pulled a face. "There's no fire, she's just got ants in her pants."

108

"Knots in her knickers," Maz joined in the teasing.

Polly ignored them. "I've got to find him," she wailed and Blanket twisted and flapped around her shoulders.

"Ooh, look at her, she's crying," Baz mocked.

"Shut up," Shaz rounded on her friend. "This is serious. She's got his blanket. He never goes anywhere without his blanket."

"They took him from school," Courtleigh explained, as he came in.

"School!" Maz made a rude noise. "I thought that's where you're supposed to be safe. Where they have rules and guards and gates and fences too high to jump over." She pursed her lips and looked down at the fashion page. "What do you think this would look like on me?"

"Like yuck," Shaz growled.

"Only asked." Maz shut her magazine. She sat up straight and suddenly no one was mocking, or teasing or bullying.

"It was that Lady Serena and her doctor, wasn't it?" Shaz said. Polly nodded.

"They've taken kids before," Maz said.

"Is that what happens to the ones that don't stay?" Courtleigh asked.

"Yeah," Baz said. "But it's never like this. It's always been like for adoption or something."

Polly gulped. "What kind of something?" The three girls looked at each other.

"We don't know," Shaz said, at last. "All we know is they never come back and no one ever says where they've gone."

Blanket went limp. Polly felt sick.

"Why don't they take you?" she said, when she was sure she was not going to throw up.

"We make ourselves as tough and horrible as we can, so no one will want us," Shaz explained.

"It's always the little ones that go first," Maz said quietly. "We try to hide them if we can, but they always find them."

"They're not having Sprog." Polly clenched her fists. "I'm going to get him back," she said fiercely. Around her shoulders Blanket gave a little wave.

The others looked at her. Baz raised her finger to her forehead to show she thought Polly was mad, then let it drop.

"I am. I just don't know where to go," Polly insisted grimly.

"We can help you with that," Shaz said.

"How?"

"We'll show you."

"When?"

"Later."

"Why not now?" Polly was bubbling with impatience. If Lady Serena was going to do something terrible to Sprog, he needed rescuing immediately.

"We've got things to do," Maz said.

"You have to wait, until we're ready, or it may not work," explained Baz.

"Midnight's the best time," Shaz said.

"That's hours away," Polly protested. The three girls ignored her.

"The Blatches will be snoring their heads off and we can get all the stuff down here," Maz said.

"Then it will be easy to get you out," said Baz.

"You mean you can get out of here?" Courtleigh cried.

"Sure," said Shaz.

"We do it all the time. You don't think we spend Saturday nights in this dump, do you?" said Maz.

"Then why do you stay?"

"Where else can we go? No one would want all three of us and we're kind of used to each other," said Baz.

"We've been together for a long time," added Shaz.

"Like the three musketeers, or the three witches, or..." Polly began.

"Shh." Shaz put a finger to her lips.

"Or the three headed dog," Courtleigh muttered, as Mrs Blatch opened the door.

Shaz threw him a murderous look, which meant. "I'll get you later."

"Supper's ready. Good wholesome food, to make you good wholesome children," Mrs Blatch trilled.

"Oooooo, she means us," Shaz shrieked and slapped Courtleigh so hard across the shoulders, that he was shoved straight into the big white wobble, that was Mrs Blatch's stomach. Teetering backwards, she grabbed hold of him to steady herself, overbalanced and as she fell, she pulled him down on top of her.

"Get him off me," she screamed. Stiffling their laughter, Maz took one arm, Baz the other and heaving Courtleigh to his feet, they dragged him away down the corridor.

Mrs Blatch lay on her back, her legs waving in the air, showing her big, white cotton knickers and her fat pink knees.

"Oh Mrs Blatch are you hurt?" Shaz knelt down beside her. "Do you need a doctor? Or an ambulance? You'll definitely need an x-ray. Should Polly go and find Mr Blatch for you?"

Mrs Blatch gave a little moan. She clutched at Shaz's arm and managed to sit up.

"Yes, fetch Herbert. I don't think anything's broken, but you can never be too sure."

"I think you should do the sensible thing and go to hospital," Shaz said firmly.

"You do?" There was a sparkle in Mrs Blatch's eye and a flush of pink on her cheek.

"I really do," Shaz nodded solemnly.

When Polly returned with Mr Blatch, he sprayed his wife from head to toe with disinfectant, then he took one arm and Shaz the other and they hoisted her to her feet.

"The car's outside dear. I've the engine running to keep it warm. We can't have you catching a chill, can we? If you can just manage to walk, we'll soon get you to the hospital," he fussed.

"But Herbert, the children. We can't leave the children," his wife wailed.

"Don't worry about us. We'll be all right," Shaz said quickly.

Mrs Blatch looked at her husband. "Perhaps we should call Scythe," she said faintly.

"And have him think we can't do our job? There's no need for that, not with this," Mr Blatch held up the big iron key to the front door. "Everything else is secure. All we have to do is lock this behind us and not even a speck of dust would be able to get out of St. Savlons."

"Yeah!" As the door clanged shut behind the Blatches, Shaz and Polly slapped palms.

"With any luck, they'll be away all night." Shaz gave a contented sigh. "So we can do anything we want." She stalked off down the corridor to the dining room, where Maz and Baz left their food and followed her without a word.

"What do we do now? Polly asked.

"Wait I suppose. Until they're ready." Courtleigh leaned over and took a potato from one of the abandoned plates. "I don't suppose Maz wants it and I'm starving."

Polly pushed her dinner to one side.

"You can have mine as well. I'm not hungry."

"You will be at midnight and it will be cold," Courtleigh said with his mouth full.

"Pig," Polly said, half heartedly.

"Gran says you've got to eat to keep your strength up."

Polly stared down at her food and wished she had a Gran, who told her what was good for her. The healthy vegetable pie and plain boiled potatoes struck in her throat, but she made an effort and managed half her dinner in the time it took Courtleigh to eat everyone else's. Then they washed up and put everything away and there were still three hours to go to midnight.

"I wish they'd hurry. Anything could be happening to Sprog," Polly said.

Courtleigh yawned and stretched. "Stay cool. There's some things you can't rush."

"I bet your Gran told you that as well," Polly snapped. He was beginning to annoy her again. Everything was beginning to annoy her and if something did not happen soon, she would explode. She put her hand up to touch her lucky charm and her fingers closed round the smooth satin edge of Blanket.

"We're ready," Maz poked her head round the kitchen door.

"But it's not time," Polly said.

Courtleigh gave a huge sigh. He jumped up and grabbed her by the arm. "If Maz says it's time, then it's time. Right?"

"Right," said Maz.

In the common room, Shaz and Baz sat cross legged on the floor. The room was dark except for four candles set around a bowl of water.

"What are you going to do?" Polly whispered.

"We look in the water and we see things," Maz replied.

"My Gran does that with a crystal ball," Courtleigh said.

"Can you tell the future?" Polly asked.

"No, but we can ask questions. Now shut up and sit down," Baz said.

"Hold hands," Shaz whispered, "and concentrate."

Polly stared hard at the unruffled surface. Maz's fingers tightened around hers, Baz drew in her breath and like a picture appearing on a screen, a building began to take shape. It was long and low like shoe box with black windows and a square front door.

"There," breathed Shaz. "That's where he is."

Baz frowned and leaned over the bowl. "I don't think it's a house."

The water wavered and the picture disappeared. Maz let go of Polly's hand and yawned. Baz rubbed her eyes. All three girls looked very tired.

"Is that it?" Polly felt sick with disappointment. Even if Shaz was right and Sprog was in that white building, none of them knew where it was.

"What more do you want?" Shaz said crossly. They all looked miserably at the bowl of water.

Then Courtleigh slapped his hand across his forehead. "It's some sort of factory, or office and I know where it is." The girls stared at him. "It's in Duke Street, where the old firework factory used to be."

Baz glanced back at the bowl as if the image was still floating in the water.

"I don't like it," she said. "Why have they taken Sprog to a factory?"

Shaz closed her eyes. She raised her palms and swayed backwards and forwards. "I don't think it is a factory. It's more like a research place; somewhere where they do experiments," she said at last.

"No one's doing anything to my brother." Polly jumped to her feet.

"Good on you!" Shaz clapped her on the shoulder. "Come on guys, we can't let this happen to Sprog."

"We've already helped. We showed her where he was," Baz yawned.

"And it's a long way away." Maz stretched her arms above her head.

"I don't care. I've got to get him," Polly cried.

"Yeah and I'm going with you," Courtleigh said. Three pairs of eyes swiveled round to look at him. "You need someone who knows the way," he shrugged.

"From here?" said Shaz doubtfully.

116

"From Gran's." Courtleigh sounded far more confident than he felt. He had never been to Gran's from St. Savlons. He had never been to this part of town before, but he thought he could probably do it and he liked the way the girls were looking at him with respect.

"OK. We'll show you how to get out. Won't we?" Shaz glared at the other two, quelling any protest with her glance.

"I think the back way's best. There are no street lights," said Maz

"What about the gates?" said Courtleigh

"We fix those," Shaz said.

On the control panel above the kitchen door, a steady green light showed that all the electronic locks were in place. Shaz and Baz stood and stared at it, while Maz went to the door and moved her hands as if drawing back the bolts and turning the key. The green light flickered, faded and grew pale. On the solid wooden door, the heavy iron bolt began to slide slowly out of its socket. Polly crossed her fingers, Courtleigh held his breath and gradually the door swung open.

"Go," said Shaz and they raced across the courtyard, squeezed through the gap in the gates and out into the street.

The cat on the roof, bunched her muscles and jumped. She landed on an outhouse, then leapt onto a wall. She took a final look at the direction in which Polly and Courtleigh had gone, then she disappeared into the shadows.

CHAPTER SIXTEEN

"We're out," Polly cried triumphantly, thrusting her fist into the air.

"Yeah well, we're not there yet. It's a long way to Duke Street," Courtleigh said.

Polly glanced behind her at the brooding shape of St. Savlons. It loomed over the wasteland of abandoned factories and broken pavements. She wanted to run as fast as she could, away from its menacing presence.

"Keep in the shadows," Courtleigh warned, as they hurried away. "We don't want anyone seeing us."

"But there's no one about." Even as she spoke a small red car swung round the corner. It bounced over the potholes, struck the kerb and juddered to a halt. The driver leaned over and opened a door.

"Polly Miller, Courtleigh Jones, get in," Jenny Abramawitch said wearily.

Polly shook her head. She planted her feet firmly on the pavement and folded her arms. Blanket wound itself tightly around her waist. Courtleigh squared his shoulders and stood beside her.

"Courtleigh," Jenny Ambramwitch's voice was like ice. Courtleigh gave a shrug and folded himself into the car. "Now you Polly."

Polly did not move. She was scared. She had never defied Miss Ambramwitch before, but no one was going to stop her finding Sprog.

On the back seat Lucy cat flicked her tail into a question mark. Jenny gave a slight shake of the head.

"Polly," she said gently. "Standing out here in the street isn't going to help anyone."

"You may as well get in," Courtleigh said miserably.

Polly gave up. Without Courtleigh's help she would never find her way to the factory.

"Traitor," she hissed as she climbed in beside him.

"What did you want me to do? If we don't do what she says, she'll get the police," he whispered.

"Yes she would," Jenny's ears were very sharp. "You shouldn't be out at this time of night. Whatever do you think you were doing?"

"We're looking for Sprog," Polly said, before Courtleigh could stop her. Jenny Abramawitch frowned, Lucy gave a warning growl. "He's disappeared. Lady Serena's got him," Polly explained. Lucy's fur bristled.

"Whatever's happened, you shouldn't be wandering about like this," Jenny said.

"But we have to find him. He's my brother."

Jenny sighed deeply. "No, Polly. He isn't. You don't have a brother. Remember what happened. Your mum disappeared after the explosion. We tried to find her, we searched everywhere. There were appeals on the TV and radio, but she never turned up. Nor did anyone else. You don't have any family, that's why you're in care."

"She could have had him after she disappeared and I never knew," Polly said defiantly. She had never thought of that before, but could be true. Sprog could be telling the truth. "It might have happened like that. It might," she insisted.

Jenny Abramawitch rested her elbows on the steering wheel and put her head in her hands. "I suppose it might," she said softly. "But now is not the time to talk about it. I've got to get you back to St. Savlons."

"We can't leave him," Polly protested.

"We can't do anything else at this time of night. I'm sure there's a perfectly good explanation for what has happened and I'll find out for you in the morning, but now you have to go back."

Polly clenched her fists. She wanted to scream and shout, but one look at the expression on Jenny's face and she clamped her teeth tightly together. Courtleigh said nothing. He stared out of the window and scowled.

When they got back to St. Savlons, lights were blazing in the windows and the gates stood wide open.

"Does that mean they know we've gone?" Polly whispered to

Courtleigh.

"Dunno. But it looks like the Blatches are back. That's their car," he whispered back. Then he turned to the social worker and said as politely as he could manage, "Please Miss Abramawitch, if we promise to go straight back in, will you let us out here? If you come in with us and tell Mr and Mrs Blatch what we've done, then they'll be upset and they've only just got back from the hospital." Jenny Abramawitch wrinkled her forehead. "Please," Courtleigh wheedled.

"If you don't trust us, you can send Lucy to make sure we do we do," Polly added.

Lucy cat gave a short, sharp miaow.

"Just this once then. But if I ever catch you out late at night again."

"You won't. We promise, don't we Polly?" Courtleigh was already sliding out of the car.

"And this time you'd better mean it," Jenny Abramawitch said sternly.

Courtleigh crossed his fingers behind his back. "Yes Mam," he said.

They slipped in through the gates and hurried round to the back door, Lucy padding silently behind them.

"Hope it's still open," Courtleigh whispered.

"What if it's not?"

"We'll be in trouble."

The kitchen lights blazed out into back yard. Courtleigh glanced at

Polly. She bit her lip as he pressed his hand against the door.

"We're OK," he breathed and they stepped inside, just as the lights went out. "Made it." Courtleigh leaned back against the wall. "Another second and we'd have been stuck outside. Mr Blatch must have just set the security system again."

It was dark in the corridors, as they crept miserably up the stairs. At the top, Courtleigh went one way, Polly another. Neither looked back, or said a word. There was nothing to say. They had failed.

CHAPTER SEVENTEEN

In the girls' dormitory, Maz sat on the bed, buffing her nails, while Shaz rubbed body lotion into her long, black legs and Baz crouched in front of the mirror patting gel under her eyes.

"What are you doing here Polly?" Shaz hissed across the room.

"Did you find him?" Maz dropped her file.

"Don't be stupid. They've not been gone long enough." Baz straightened up. She put the top back on the jar and asked, "so what went wrong?"

Faces shiny with night cream, the three girls settled themselves on Polly's bed and listened as she told them how they had been caught by Miss Abramawitch.

"How did she know?" Shaz mused.

"What do you mean?" Polly said.

"Well we didn't know what we were going to do until we did it, but there she was in the middle of the night in the right place at the right time."

"Like she always is," added Maz.

"She always knows when something's going on," said Baz.

"I wish she knew what was going on with Sprog," said Polly.

"She does," said Maz.

Polly shook her head. "No, she doesn't. She said she'd find out in the morning and tell me, but it might be too late by then."

"You're right. If Miss A doesn't know, then something very weird is going on," said Shaz. Polly bit her lip. "It's OK." Shaz saw her distress. "You and Courtleigh can have another go tomorrow."

"But we can't wait til tomorrow night."

"You don't have to. We'll sort it. Watch."

Courtleigh was lying on his bed, staring into the dark. He hadn't bothered to wash or undress. He did not want to switch on the light and see the rows of empty beds, all neatly made, as if no one had ever slept in them.

"Courtleigh."

The door opened and his name wafted into the room, as if carried by the breeze. He sat up and rubbed his eyes. Even in the dark, he could see there was no one there.

"Courtleigh." It came again, more insistently this time.

Courtleigh slapped the side of his head, trying to clear the noises out of his brain. The corridor was empty, but he could see a faint line of light at the far end, which seemed to be coming from the girls' room. Were they calling him? No. They couldn't be. And in any case it was forbidden to go into the girls' dormitory. He lay back on his pillow and closed his eyes.

"Courtleigh Jones, come here this minute," the voice screeched through him like nails sliding down a blackboard.

"If you don't we'll fry your brain," another voice chipped in.

"We can do it. Just try us," the third voice sounded suspiciously like Baz.

"OK. OK. Stay cool," Courtleigh muttered, as he swung off the bed and hurried down the corridor to the girls' dormitory.

"What took you so long?" Shaz said.

"It would have been quicker to come and get you," Baz complained.

"I don't think we've got it quite right yet," Maz said.

"It's not us. It's him. He's not sensitive enough," said Shaz.

"Then we'll have to train him," Baz threatened. "Grab him and hold him down."

"I'm going." Courtleigh put his hands up and began backing away.

"Not if you want to find Sprog," said Shaz.

"OK, but you have to keep off me." Courtleigh looked at them warily.

"Right," said Shaz. "This is what we're going to do."

In the morning Mrs Blatch was feeling a little frail. Her arm was still in a sling. The doctor had said it wasn't really necessary, but she felt that when it came to your health, you could never be too careful. The visit to the hospital had been very successful. While she and Mr Blatch had waited in the Emergency Department, they had seen a number of very nasty injuries and learned about all sorts of interesting diseases. When they returned to St. Savlons, Mr Blatch wanted to fumigate the place immediately, but Mrs Blatch persuaded him to wait until the children had gone to school, before starting a full scale disinfecting process.

"It won't be long now, Herbert," she said, glancing up at the kitchen clock. "The school bus will be here in five minutes."

"I'll just pop into the dining room and hurry them up." Mr Blatch adjusted his glasses and trotted down the corridor, spray in hand.

Polly and Courtleigh were at one table, Baz, Shaz and Maz at another. They sat with their heads bowed in total silence. As he opened the door, Shaz and said in a tearful voice,

"Mr Blatch don't come any further."

"It's too terrible," Maz groaned, her eyes swimming.

"It's very, very catching," Baz sobbed.

Mr Blatch gulped. He raised his spray. The three girls turned their faces towards him. He swayed; the can fell from his trembling hands and he turned and ran from the room screaming,

"Emergency, emergency. Get a doctor. Ring for an ambulance."

Mrs Blatch heard the panic in his voice and hurried out of the kitchen.

"Herbert whatever is it?" she cried.

"Oh my dear," he gasped. "It's the girls. They're covered. There are big black spots all over their faces."

"Spots! Herbert pull yourself together. All teenagers have spots."

"Not like these. You've never seen any like these."

"Nonsense." Mrs Blatch pushed past her hysterical husband and flung open the dining room door. She took one look at the pustulating pimples that were rapidly spreading over the weeping girls and staggered back.

"Mrs Blatch, please help us," Shaz whimpered.

"We were all right when we went to bed and look at us now." Maz stumbled to her feet and held out her arms. From her wrists to her elbows, spots seeped green gunge.

"Don't touch me," gasped Mrs Blatch. "Don't move. Stay there."

"But we need help," moaned Baz.

"Yes, yes, of course. Help is on its way. Mr Blatch is ringing for it, at this very moment. Just don't move, don't breathe, don't do anything."

"We won't. We feel too ill," groaned Shaz.

"Oh my," Mrs Blatch took in great gulps of air.

"I think it's a new virus," Shaz moaned. She laid her head on her arms, revealing another crop of pustules on the back of her neck.

Outside St. Savlons, the school bus was forced on to the pavement, as three ambulances, sirens blaring and lights flashing tore through the open gates. Paramedics, completely covered in protective suits, raced up the steps and in through the front door.

"They're in here," Mr Blatch waved wildly at the dining room.

"Save us, please save us," Shaz cried.

She staggered from her chair with her arms outstretched, took one step and crumpled to the floor. Baz tried desperately to reach her friend, but her legs gave way. Maz fell back against the wall and slid into a faint.

Minutes later three bodies strapped onto stretchers were carried out of the building. As the ambulances left, another vehicle with the words "Contamination Unit" painted in red on its sides, swept in. Mr Blatch screamed out directions; Mrs Blatch held a tissue to her face and moaned, while Courtleigh and Polly slipped quietly out of the gate.

CHAPTER EIGHTEEN

"That's done then. We've been up to the attics and down to the cellars. You won't find any bugs lurking in St. Savlons. I'd stake my reputation on it." The head of the Contamination Unit held out his clip board to Mr Blatch. "If you could sign here, please, we'll be on our way. We've got a very interesting case of grasshoppers at the Sow and Grow Garden Produce Supermarket in Smith Street."

"Grasshoppers," Mr Blatch clicked his teeth. "I didn't know they spread germs."

"Oh yes," the contamination man nodded his head sagely. "Everything spreads germs, as you know only too well Mr Blatch."

They were settling down to a very interesting conversation about germs, microbes and viruses and all the terrible diseases they could cause, when Mrs Blatch's voice floated through the open door.

"Herbert," she called, "have the other two been done?"

"We've done all the rooms," the man with the clipboard said.

"I don't mean the rooms, I mean the children," Mrs Blatch tottered into the room.

"What children?"

"That um and hmm," Mrs Blatch waved a hand in the air. "The girl and the boy," she said in exasperation. She rarely took the trouble to learn anyone's name. Except for Shaz, Baz and Maz, no one ever stayed long enough at St. Savlons to make it worth her while.

The man with the clip board scratched his head and frowned. "Sorry," he said, "I haven't seen any children. Don't know anything about any children. Children are not on my job specification."

Eyes wide with horror, Mr and Mrs Blatch stared at each other. "Oh Herbert, where have they gone? Do you think they can be out there somewhere, spreading this deadly virus throughout the whole country?"

"I don't know, my dear," Mr Blatch was wringing his hands, his glasses had slipped to the end of his nose and his face was shiny with distress. "But we have to find them."

The man with the clipboard looked very stern. "I should think so too," he said. "You can't have anyone with those sort of germs wandering about. They could be spreading plague, infection and contamination."

"I know, I know," Mrs Blatch moaned. "What can we do?"

"Don't ask me. I can't help you. As I said children are not part of the job specification. You'll have to notify the authorities and let them deal with it. Otherwise you could be responsible for a full scale emergency."

Mr and Mrs Blatch nodded miserably.

As the van drove out of the gates, Mr Blatch turned to his wife.

"I'll call Scythe."

"Must you?" she said fearfully. She took hold of his arm to steady herself.

"Oh Herbert, he'll think we can't do our job and then what will happen to us?"

"I know my dear, but we don't want to get the police involved do we? They'll be sure to ask awkward questions. And we have to get the two of them back. We can't risk a mass epidemic, can we? No. It will be all right. He'll find them. You know what he's like, when he's on the scent, he'll follow it to the death."

Mrs Blatch went to her office, trembling from head to foot. A line of pills stood on the desk, but her hand shook too much to pick up the glass of water she needed to swallow them. A new virus had been discovered at St. Savlons, a world first. It was too exciting. It had already been on the morning news and there was a special report scheduled for the lunch time bulletin. If only those two children had not gone missing, this would be one of the best days of her life. She stared at the pills and wondered which one she should take first. She had just decided that a tranquilizer was what she needed most, when with a dark clang, the door bell began to toll. Mrs Blatch's hands flew to her chest.

"Oh thank goodness, that must be Scythe. Though how he's got in I can't imagine. Herbert, you must have forgotten to shut the gates," she called, as she hurried to open the door.

"May I come in?" Jenny Abramwitch stood on the doorstep. Mrs Blatch suddenly felt very odd.

"No, no, you can't. This is an infected zone. The virus started here and I think I might have caught it too. You have to go away. Now this minute." She flapped her hands in the direction of the gates, but Jenny stood her ground.

"I came to see if Polly and Courtleigh were all right," she said.

"Yes, yes, they are quite all right. Both of them. Quite well," Mrs Blatch flustered.

"Then they've gone to school?"

"Yes. No. Of course not." Mrs Blatch took a deep breath and with it came inspiration. "They are in quarantine. So you can't see them."

"But you said they weren't ill."

"No. I mean yes. I mean. Oh dear, I think I might be going to faint." Mrs Blatch staggered backwards and as she did so, she clutched at the door handle. As it closed behind her, Lucy cat trotted round from the back of the building.

"Did you see them?" Jenny asked.

The cat shook her head. Jenny knelt down and Lucy put her paws on her shoulders. Their foreheads touched and they stayed very still for a moment or two, then with a flick of her tail the cat was away.

"Find them, Lucy, find them," Jenny called. "And I'll try and find out what Scythe is up to."

It did not take Lucy long to pick up the trail. She travelled over walls and along rooftops. In front of her, spread out like a map, lay a warren of back yards, intersecting alleyways and wide tree lined roads. Sometimes she had to scramble to the top of a roof to get her bearings, but eventually she found them, sitting on the steps of an empty house in Albert Street. Her tail twitched and she was steadying herself for the jump onto the next roof, when a black van appeared at the end of the road.

There was nothing she could do. They were too far away. The van was getting closer. It was slowing. Then a bike shot out of a side street, without looking. Scythe swerved to avoid it and slid straight past the two children.

There was still time to warn them. Lucy walked carefully down the slope of the roof, then jumped two stories and landed neatly on a garden wall. An angry dog lunged at her, barking and growling. Lucy gave a disdainful flick of the tail, turned and came face to face with a huge orange tom cat. Fur bristling, tail vibrating, he was poised to attack. The Siamese yowled; she unsheathed her claws and sprang.

The battle was short and fierce. Lucy cat went straight for the throat, sinking her teeth deep into her opponent's flesh. She followed with a swipe from the left and a swipe from the right and the orange cat fled, howling with fear.

A stray bite had caught her ear, but there was no time to do more than give it a quick lick, before she was on her way. Easing herself down onto the ground, she bounded along the alley. When she reached the road, she saw no sign of the black van. Scythe had gone, but so had Polly and Courtleigh. Hoping she was not too late, she raced towards Gran's.

CHAPTER NINETEEN

"Are we nearly there?" Polly wanted to know.

"Yeah," Courtleigh said. He looked anxiously across the maze of garden walls and back alleys and wondered how long it would be before he had to admit that he was lost. Polly followed his gaze.

"I think we've been down this way before."

"No, we haven't," Courtleigh said hotly.

Polly looked at him. "You don't know where we are, do you?"

"I do. It's just that all the houses round here look the same."

"Now what are we going to do?" Polly said miserably. She shifted the straps of her rucksack and Blanket poked out an edge and stroked her gently on the cheek.

"I told you. It will be OK. Victoria Road's here, or in the next road." Courtleigh waved his hand in what he hoped was the direction of Gran's house.

Polly bit her lip. She knew they were lost, but what else could she do but follow Courtleigh?

He strode away and she stumbled after him, her eyes glued to his back in case he made a sudden turn or dived down yet another alley. She was getting more and more tired and it was harder and harder to concentrate. It was like running through porridge. Her legs were too heavy to lift and now her feet were tangled round something soft. She kicked out to stop herself falling and as she staggered back into the hedge, the plump black cat that was winding itself round her ankles gave a very offended miaow. Polly grabbed hold of a clump of privet and managed to stop herself from sitting down on the pavement. The cat stared at her with round yellow eyes.

"Go away," Polly snarled.

The cat nipped the bottom of her jeans, then trotted down the pavement and twined itself round Courtleigh's legs, until he was forced to stop. He crouched down to look at it, then sprang up, throwing his arms into the air.

"Hey man, here's Nemesis, Gran's cat. I told you we were nearly there. All we've got to do is follow him."

"I don't want to go to your Gran's. I want to get Sprog back," Polly said mutinously.

Courtleigh's stomach rumbled. His throat was dry and his feet were sore. "We can go there first. Get something to eat and drink."

"But Sprog's in danger," Polly protested.

Courtleigh shrugged. "I know. But what can we do in the middle of the day? You can't go up to the front door and say, "Please Lady Serena can I have my brother back." We've got to wait 'til it's dark."

"Then we'll go?"

"Sure. That's what we came for, isn't it. Come on. Gran's probably got the bacon frying already."

Polly clenched her fists. She knew Courtleigh was right, but she did not want to go to his Gran's. She didn't like families. Whenever she had tried to live with one, it had always ended in disaster. She never knew what to do, or what to say and they always made it plain that they did not want her in their home.

Home was something she knew nothing about. She did not understand how it worked. She had never lived in a place where people were warm and caring. She had never even visited friends from school, because she had never been at any school long enough to make the sort of friends, who asked you home.

Gran was waiting for them at the door. Her face wrinkled with concern, as she saw how Courtleigh loped eagerly up the path, but Polly hung back, unsure of her welcome. .

"Come on in. It will be done in a minute," she called, as a wonderful smell of bacon frying wafted down the hallway.

Courtleigh looked at Polly. "See," he whispered.

"See what?" Gran demanded.

"I told her you'd have breakfast ready," Courtleigh said sheepishly.

"So I have and there's no need to whisper about it. It's bad manners.

You're forgetting what I told you about always keeping a polite tongue in your head to keep you out of trouble."

"Yes Gran. Sorry Gran," Courtleigh said, but he was grinning.

"You're a good boy." Gran stood on tiptoe and gave him a quick kiss on the cheek.

Then she turned to Polly. Her bright black eyes twinkled. "You're a good girl too. A good friend to my Courtleigh and always welcome in my house."

Polly beamed. Bubbles of happiness fizzed inside her. Her feet didn't hurt any more and she had to stop herself from skipping with joy, as they followed Gran into the kitchen, where the round table was already laid with two sets of knives and forks; bacon sizzled in a pan and a tea pot steamed on the range. They sat down and Gran poured them mugs of strong tea, which she sweetened with condensed milk. Polly took one sip and felt the delicious sweetness slide down her throat. Gran fried ackees and tomatoes and scallions and piled their plates high.

"Pickapepper sauce?" she asked.

Courtleigh nodded, happily. "It's very hot," he warned, but Polly was willing to try anything. She had never seen food like this before, but if Courtleigh's Gran had cooked it, she was sure it was going to be delicious.

After three platefuls and a pile of toast and honey, Courtleigh leaned back and gave a contented sigh.

"Now," said Gran "you can get on with the dishes." Polly pushed back her chair, but Gran put her hand on her arm. "Not you Polly. You sit with me for a while."

Polly looked at Courtleigh expecting a fuss, but he just grinned and loading their dirty plates onto a tray, took them out into the scullery.

"Let me look at your hand chile," Gran said.

"What for?"

"To see what's there."

Polly looked down at her palm. "There's nothing but bumps and lines."

"That's what I'm going to look at."

Gran drew her chair closer and took Polly's hand. She studied it for a long time. Polly heard the cat going out of the cat flap, the hiss of hot water in the sink and the clink of plates being stacked on the draining board, then at last Gran said, "I know you."

A shiver slithered up Polly's spine. "I knew your mum before she disappeared."

Polly dug her nails into the palm of her hand. Her mouth was dry and a pulse was beating in her throat.

"And my dad?" she croaked.

Gran shook her head. "He wasn't around."

Polly swallowed. "You mean my dad's still alive?" Lips pursed, Gran nodded briefly. "Then why didn't he come and find me?" she said shakily.

139

"He didn't know about you. Your Mum never told him," Gran said shortly. She peered again at Polly's outstretched palm. "You know, you are a very lucky girl. Only three of you were saved from that explosion, you, your mum and my Courtleigh. His mum didn't make it."

Gran screwed up her eyes and took another look. "You were saved by your guardian. Without him you would have been burned to death."

"My what?" Polly asked incredulously. For the first time in her life, she had learned something new about her family. Somewhere out in the world, she had a father and now there was a guardian. Was it an uncle or an aunt? Whoever it was, it was someone who cared. Or at least had cared enough at the time, to save her life. Maybe they had been blown up too. After all Gran had only mentioned three people being saved. She leaned forward eagerly, hoping to learn more, when with a bang and a swing of the cat flap, a screaming and howling Nemesis tore into the room and skidded to a halt in front of Gran.

She dropped Polly's hand and bent her head to listen to his urgent squeaking and mewing and growling. He had scarcely finished, when she leapt from her chair.

"You've got to go. He's here." There was a heavy knock at the front door. "Go now. Out the back. I'll hold him for as long as I can."

Polly grabbed her rucksack and she and Courtleigh ran out of the kitchen, but the tiny back garden was surrounded on all sides by high brick walls.

"We can't get out," Polly cried. Courtleigh looked round desperately for something they could climb on, but already they could hear Scythe's voice, smooth and oily saying,

"I know they are here. I can smell them. You wouldn't be stupid enough to hide them in the house, so perhaps the back yard would be a good place to look."

It was all over. There was a cold sick feeling in the pit of Polly's stomach. Now they would never find Sprog. He would be lost for ever, like all the other children who had disappeared from St. Savlons. And what about her mum and dad? They would never know about her.

"Come on." Courtleigh grabbed her hand.

"There's nowhere to go," Polly was close to tears.

"Shut your eyes," Courtleigh hissed. "And fall." He tugged at her arm; her knees gave way and she was falling and falling and falling.

CHAPTER TWENTY

Polly's feet bumped against the ground. She smelled earth and rotting leaves.

"We made it," she cried.

Courtleigh grinned. "Yeah man. I did it. We're in The Edges. Scythe will never find us here. Come on."

"Where are we going?"

"Dunno. Doesn't matter. Got to get away from here. Then we'll think about getting out."

The tunnels were dark and it was hard to see, but after a while their eyes adjusted to the dimness. At first it was as if they were walking through a huge pipe, the walls and floor were smooth and their footsteps echoed around them. Then the pipe ended and now the ground was beaten of earth and the roots of trees made a tangled ceiling above their heads. Neither of them worried about Scythe, but Polly listened out for the Scooper and the Night People.

Courtleigh was less cautious. He strode along, humming under his breath, feeling very pleased with himself, for he had opened the way into

The Edges not once, but twice. He had outwitted Scythe and he was on his way to rescue Sprog. Gran would be so proud of him.

After about half an hour they reached a branch in the tunnels.

"Where do we go now?" Polly asked. She was thirsty, her legs ached. It was hours and hours since they had escaped from St. Savlons and they had still not reached the place, where Sprog was being held.

"Stay cool, I'll find the way," Courtleigh said. Polly looked doubtful. "I got us to Gran's, didn't I?"

"Nemesis got us to Gran's," she muttered under her breath.

Courtleigh glanced down one tunnel, then the next. There seemed to be no difference between them so he decided to take the right hand one. The floor of this tunnel was soft and sandy and in places there were alcoves cut out of the walls, which reminded Polly of the den, where the Night People had taken her. Every few steps she would stop and sniff, but the air stayed sweet.

"Round the next corner, we'll stop for a bit," Courtleigh said. He looked at his watch. "No sweat. It's not night yet."

Polly nodded and yawned, thinking how good it would be to curl up and sleep for a while. Courtleigh chose a place where the tunnel wall curved inwards and they settled down, side by side. Polly's eyes were closing, her head was growing heavy. Blanket slid out the rucksack and curled around her knees. Courtleigh leaned back against the soft side of the tunnel and tipped his baseball cap over his eyes. Polly leaned against his shoulder, his head rested on hers and they slept.

Back in the house, Gran drew herself up and focusing her powers, began to weave a web of protection. A ribbon of electric blue light crackled around the door frame. Sparks shot across the gap and thickened into tendrils of the finest steel, which hardened into a dense mesh across the doorway.

Scythe raised his hand, muttered a single word and the mesh crumpled. "Stupid woman," he said scornfully. "Did you think this would hold me? You who are old and weak thought you had power over me. If I had time, I would teach you what it means to tangle with Scythe, but for now all I want is those children."

He strode out into the back yard. His footsteps clanging on the stone flags, as he searched every corner, while Nemesis wickered with fear and Gran trawled desperately through her memory for any spell that might bind the evil swirling around her house.

"Where are they?" In spite of her efforts to keep them out, Scythe's eyes burned deep into her mind. "Tell me old woman. You know you can't hide anything from Scythe."

Gran made herself think of sunlight, of the bright white light sparkling on the sea around the island where she was born.

"I will know. You know I will," his voice hissed.

Gran thought of tall blue mountains and deep green forest. It was no good. She sensed Scythe towering over her. Felt his coldness surrounding her. She could no longer hold the pictures in her mind and, as the flame trees with their orange flowers shriveled, she saw a tunnel deep under the ground, where the walls were beaten earth and a tangle of roots formed the ceiling. There were ruins of houses set in the sides and a faint smell of rotting leaves.

"Ah ha! I should have known," Scythe's triumphant voice shattered the image. "They've gone to The Edges. So they are no ordinary children. Excellent. Oh how Lady Serena will enjoy working on them." He turned on his heel and strode out of the house.

Gran put her head in her hands and wept. She had failed. All her life she had been the one people turned to when they were in trouble. She had cast spells for the lovelorn, charmed warts and granted wishes. She had been the strong one, protecting first her only son, then her beloved grandson and now she had betrayed him and poor little Polly too.

The cat flap flicked. Nemesis got up from his place at Gran's feet. His whiskers shook, his fur trembled, but he was determined to be brave. Nervously, he peered round the door of the scullery. Then, with a yelp of recognition, he ran to greet Lucy cat. They stood forehead to forehead for a moment, then Lucy padded purposefully into the kitchen. She leapt onto the table and nudged and fussed and whickered, until at last Gran looked up.

"They've gone. I've lost them," Gran wept. Lucy's tail curled into a question mark. "They went into The Edges. It's my fault. I always told

Courtleigh that was where he had to go if anything bad happened."

Lucy put her face up to Gran's and as their foreheads touched, Gran saw Scythe going down into the tunnels. Lucy's fur bristled. Her tail snaked from side to side. Gran shook her head. Lucy yowled and nipped her finger.

"All right all right." Gran got heavily to her feet. "I'll show you the way, but I don't see what good you can do."

Lucy jumped down from the table. She twisted herself around Gran's ankles, round and round, purring and twining, until Gran felt the heaviness of her grief lift from her shoulders. She bent down to give her a grateful pat, but Lucy was already at the back door.

Out in the yard, Gran raised her face to the sky and began to chant. Her eyes closed. She held out her arms and her body swayed and her feet pounded the earth in response to the drum beat she heard in her heart. In front of her, the paving stones began to shrink and a hole opened in the ground. Lucy peered over the edge into the darkness, then she waved her tail and jumped.

CHAPTER TWENTY ONE

Scythe did not possess a key. Entry into the half world of The Edges was not among his many skills and powers. However, he knew another way of getting in. He parked the van in a side street and made his way into the Underground station. Instinctively the few people, who were waiting for the next train, avoided the tall man in the dark hat and coat and no one noticed as he stepped off the end of the platform and slid his way into a service tunnel.

There were only one or two lights, but Scythe had no problem seeing in the dark.

His eyes glowed, as he ran a hand over the rough brick of the wall and his fingers found the jagged, crack which would allow him to enter The Edges.

As he stepped into the underworld, he lifted his face and sniffed. They were very close, so close he could smell them. How he hated the sickly, sweet, stink of human children. How glad he was that his blood was pure, that his family could trace an unbroken line back to the great Archangel himself.

He slipped silently through the tunnels, his eyes red as coals and there they were curled up together as pure and innocent as the first two people on earth. Scythe's yellow tongue flickered over his purple lips. His tall figure stooped over the sleeping children. He stretched out his hand.

Meanwhile, Lucy cat had landed in The Edges. Her eyes adjusted instantly to the blackness and she quickly picked up Polly and Courtleigh's scent. Overlaying it was a deeper, darker odour, that made the hackles rise on the back of her neck and told her that Scythe was already here and that she had to find the children before he did.

She hurried through the tunnels, her nostrils quivering as the air began to grow thick with the stink of rotting fish. Suddenly a pack of black shapes swooped out of the darkness. Spitting and cursing, they waved strange misshapen limbs, as they circled her.

"Get her, beat her, bite her, suck her blood," they spat and snarled.

Lucy cat tensed, arched her back and hissed. The crowd parted. A huge woman wearing a turban lumbered towards her.

"What a pretty little cat," Mad Magda cried. Lucy yowled. Lowering herself on her haunches, she sprang straight onto Magda's shoulders. Digging her nails into the mountain of soft flesh, she bent her head towards the woman's ear, hissing softly, while the Night People waited uneasily for their leader to tell them what to do.

"Scythe's here!" Mad Magda shrieked suddenly. "We'll get him, we'll tear him."

The cat leapt to the ground and holding her tail like a banner she led the Night People through the darkness.

Scythe's shadow crouched over the sleeping children, as Lucy rounded the corner.

The cat howled and flung herself on his back, sinking her claws deep into his flesh.

"Now we've got the slimy Scythe, let's show him," hissed the dog headed man.

"Tear him, beat him," growled Boyd.

"Bite him, scratch him," Lakey screeched.

"Pay him back for what he did to us." Cassie wound a scaly tail around Scythe's neck.

"Squeeze the living daylights out of him," Mad Magda howled.

"No," Scythe screamed, his face white with terror. Half asleep, Polly and Courtleigh stumbled to their feet. Polly grabbed her rucksack and as Blanket slid itself under the flap, Courtleigh seized her hand and they ran and ran, until the sound of the fight faded into the distance.

"Those Night People, they don't look human, man," Courtleigh said, leaning back against the wall and taking deep breaths. Polly collapsed beside him gasping and panting.

"I think they were once, but Scythe did something to them," Polly managed. "Come on. We mustn't stop. If he did that to them, what's he going to do to Sprog?"

Courtleigh shrugged. "I don't think Mr Scythe is going to be doing anything to anyone ever again."

"But there's still Lady Serena. She's something to do with this and she's the one that's got him." Polly was dancing with impatience.

"Stay cool, man. No one's following us, so that's OK, but we have to figure out where we are. There's hundreds of these tunnels. If we keep running, we might end up miles from where we want to be and it will take even longer to get Sprog."

"Yes, but where are we?"

"I don't know yet. I've got to think."

"This is stupid," Polly growled. She had had enough of Courtleigh pretending he knew where they were going. She wanted to get out of The Edges and she wanted to find Sprog. Furiously, she stamped down the nearest tunnel.

"Wait for me. You've got the torch." Courtleigh hurried after her. Keeping her back to him, Polly peered into the darkness.

"I know where we are," she said.

"Where?"

"Jocelyn's." Polly pointed to the purple door glowing in the darkness.

"So what?"

"He can tell us the way out," Polly said.

"I suppose." Courtleigh was doubtful.

Polly shot him a baleful glance and rapped loudly on the door. There was a long, long wait. Somewhere in the distance, they could hear the first faint whisper of the Scooper. If it came down this tunnel, they would have to run. Courtleigh was already bouncing on the balls of his feet, preparing to sprint, when Polly knocked again, the door opened and Jocelyn appeared leaning against the frame. He wore a silk dressing gown and was very pale. In one hand he held his inhaler.

"Do come in," he whispered.

"Are you all right?" Polly asked.

Jocelyn waved a limp hand. "Just weary. Oh so weary." He sank down on the purple cushion and closed his eyes. "They make me work so hard," he breathed.

Courtleigh made a face at Polly. Jocelyn opened one eye. "They do," he insisted faintly.

Polly sat down beside him. "Who makes you work?"

"Oh you don't want to know."

"Yes, I do." Gazing at him, she leaned forward, resting her chin on her hand. Courtleigh scowled. Once Jocelyn started, Polly would want to sit there listening to his stories for ages. Sticking his hands in his pockets, he wandered round the room.

"If I don't do as they say, I don't get any food." Tears sparkled on Jocelyn's lashes.

"I don't know how they can treat me like this. I belong to one of the oldest families. The very best." His voice shook. He gave a deep sigh and there was a hint of brimstone in the air.

The curtain of bottle tops rattled, as Courtleigh pushed his head into the kitchen.

Jocelyn's eyes flew open.

"Sit down. You're making me nervous," he snapped.

"I was just looking. It's cool man."

Jocelyn fluttered his eye lashes. "It is good, isn't it. I did it all myself. It's my own design. You won't find anything like it anywhere. Would you like the guided tour?"

"Yes please," Polly said.

Jocelyn unfolded himself and rose to his feet. "You must understand that this is only my pied-a-terre, my little place where I can get away and be alone. My family has homes all over the world, but I'm rather fond of my little den."

He peered at them intently to see if they believed him. Polly nodded vigorously, Courtleigh shrugged.

"Here I can indulge my creative talent, you see." Jocelyn waved a hand and Polly and Courtleigh looked round at the bits of glass and foil set into the walls and suspended from the ceiling.

"It's beautiful," Polly said.

Jocelyn simpered. "It is, isn't it. Now for the rest of my cave." He pushed aside the bottle top curtain and they stepped into a small, very old fashioned kitchen. There was a stone sink, shelves crammed with china and a four legged stove.

"And now my party trick." Jocelyn puckered up his mouth and blew. Plumes of gas shot from the burners. Blue, yellow and orange light danced on the ceiling and flickered round the walls. Polly clapped her hands in delight. Jocelyn preened and bowed.

"Next, my inner sanctum. This way if you please." The bathroom shimmered with glass. There were mirrors everywhere. Jocelyn leaned towards the one over the basin.

"Dear me, I look terrible. At least a hundred and eight." He glanced down at his dressing gown and gave a little shiver. "I don't think this colour does anything for me."

"I think it makes you look very..." Polly began.

"Very elegant," Jocelyn finished. "Mm, I think you could be right." He twirled round and smiled at his reflection. "Well, now that I've shown you my little hideaway, you must sit down and tell me what you've been up to, since I last saw you."

Jocelyn settled himself on his purple cushion. Polly sat down beside him, but Courtleigh remained standing. Jocelyn looked at him, but he did not move. Ignoring him Jocelyn turned to Polly.

"I must admit I didn't think I would ever see you again."

"We got lost," Polly said.

"And you found me. How delightful." Jocelyn patted her arm, then his eyes flew open. "Don't tell me you've been wandering around down here all this while," he cried.

"Oh no. Mr Scythe…" Polly began.

There was a loud rattle from the direction of the kitchen. Jocelyn coughed loudly. A wisp of smoke rose from his nostrils. The noise came again, louder this time.

"What was that?" Courtleigh said.

"Nothing you need know anything about," Jocelyn said abruptly. He turned his attention to Polly. "What was it you were saying about Mr Scythe?"

"He found me in the tunnels," Polly began again.

In the kitchen something crashed to the floor. Jocelyn frowned, but made no move to go and see what had happened.

"I think something's broken." Courtleigh stepped back and pushed his way through the bottle top curtain. Instantly, Jocelyn was on his feet. In the kitchen, everything was the same as they had left it.

"You see," Jocelyn said, "nothing's happened."

"But I heard it," Courtleigh persisted.

"Perhaps it came from there," Polly said helpfully, pointing to a door at the opposite side of the room.

Jocelyn waved his hand about. "No, no that's just a cupboard." There was another crash. "Believe me, there's nothing there. Only mops and

154

brooms. You go and sit down and I'll get you a drink and a biscuit. You poor things, you must be simply famished after your journey. I've got ginger snaps and chili biscuits and fiery tacs," he continued, trying desperately to get them out of the kitchen.

Inside what Jocelyn insisted was a cupboard, Courtleigh could hear banging against the bars of a cage and he remembered what Podner had said about never trusting a shape changer. Something, or someone, needed help. If he could get Polly to distract Jocelyn, then he could slip through that door, but she was crazy about dragons and would never believe that Jocelyn was keeping someone prisoner in his back room.

Polly put her hand up to touch her lucky charm. There was something very strange going on. Jocelyn had shown them round his den, why wouldn't he show them what was making all that noise? Suddenly, she had an idea. She walked over to the sink.

"I'm very thirsty. Can I have a drink of water?"

"Water!" Jocelyn screwed up his nose, as if the thought was quite disgusting. "Wouldn't you rather have ginger beer? It's got more zzzzz to it."

"Please," Polly said politely.

"Water or ginger?"

"Yes."

"You're getting me confused," he complained.

"Sorry. I'd like water." Polly turned the tap on full. Just as she hoped, water bounced off the sink and fell in bright drops onto the floor. "No. I think I want ginger beer instead," she said.

"Really. Can't you make up your mind?" Jocelyn said peevishly. "Oh well, if that's what you want I've got a bottle in here somewhere." He turned round and peered into a cupboard.

As he did so, Courtleigh leaned back and pressed down hard on the handle. The door opened and he slipped inside. The room, that Jocelyn had said was a cupboard, was   lined with cages. They were all empty, except one.

"Took you long enough to come and get me," Podner said.

Courtleigh looked at the padlock. "Where's the key?"

"'E's got it. That jumped up creature what thinks 'e's someone. It's in 'is pocket."

In the kitchen, the water from the sink was puddling all over the ground. Polly sloshed it about with her feet, while Jocelyn searched for the ginger beer.

"Has it got lots of bubbles?" she asked.

"What?"

"The ginger beer. I only like it with lots of bubbles."

"Of course it's got bubbles." Jocelyn's hand closed round a bottle.

"Lots and lots of bubbles?" Polly glanced anxiously at the door. "I like them so fizzy that my nose tickles."

"You really are a most annoying little girl."

The door opened. "He's got Podner in there," Courtleigh cried.

Holding the bottle of ginger beer like a weapon, Jocelyn spun round. Polly dodged to one side, he followed and as she had planned, his feet slipped on the wet floor. He put out a hand to save himself, dropping the bottle. Glass shattered, ginger beer fizzed and as green blood spurted from a jagged gash of his arm. Jocelyn screamed.

"Help! I'm dying. I can't stand the sight of blood. I'm going to faint."

"The key is in his pocket," Courtleigh cried.

Jocelyn closed his eyes. "My inhaler, get my inhaler, before it's too late," he moaned.

"I'll get it." Polly thrust her hand into a dressing gown pocket. Her fingers closed round the inhaler and the key beneath it. "I'm sorry. I can't find it," she lied.

Jocelyn took a great shuddering gasp. "I can't breathe. There is so much blood."

"I saw it in the other room. Keep still, I'll go and get it," Polly cried. She tossed the key to Courtleigh and they ran into the back room.

Podner rattled the bars. "'Urry up, can't you," he snapped, as Courtleigh put the key in the lock. Polly's hand closed round her lucky charm.

"Come on," she whispered. She could hear Jocelyn moaning and thrashing about. Courtleigh gave a final twist. The door of the cage swung open and Podner jumped into her arms. She held him tightly, as they raced back through the kitchen.

They were almost through the curtain, when Jocelyn opened one eye. It glowed black, then red with fury. His body expanded, took on his dragon shape, smoke rose from his nostrils and his tail began to thrash. The cave shook. Pots crashed from shelves, china shattered on the ground. In the living room strands of foil were torn from the ceiling. The dragon's breath scorched their backs. Podner buried his face in Polly's jumper. Courtleigh flung open the front door. As they burst out a plume of flame lit up the tunnel.

"Rats!" The dragon's body stuck, half in and half out of the purple door. Its eyes bulged, its tail beat against the walls in a frantic effort to free itself.

Podner lifted his head and looked back over Polly's shoulder.

"Stupid creature," he said.

The dragon heaved and shoved. The door frame groaned and creaked. Wood splintered, as the purple door tore from its hinges. Hot, fiery tears splashed to the ground. There was a great roar of despair, then the dragon's scales shriveled and a pale young man slumped against the wall. Jocelyn looked at the ruins of his room and rubbed the tears from his eyes. He reached into his pocket for his handkerchief and found his inhaler. The girl had lied. It had been there all the time. But the key had gone.

He ran through his flooded kitchen. The door to the workroom stood open, the cage was empty. Fear bumped about in his chest. When they came to fetch the creature and found it was gone, they would be very, very angry. Then what would they do to him? Would they take him away? Would they use him for their experiments? They'd only let him stay down here, because he was so useful. Any strange or half changed things the Scooper picked up, he would keep, until they were sent for.

Jocelyn began to shake. His skin grew coarse, his face lengthened, his body swelled, smoke spiraled from his nostrils. Then abruptly the changing stopped. However hard he tried to concentrate, to make himself think of leaping flames and molten lava, it was no good, he was stuck. In spite of coming from one of the oldest families, he'd never managed to get this shape changing thing right. That was why he had to live down here in The Edges. Jocelyn looked down at the scales that covered the back of his hands and gave a large, wet sob. He was no better than the Night People.

He sank down on the purple cushion and hid his face in his arms. After a while, his shape began to waver. His body shrank, his scales faded, he tucked his knees up to his chin and covered his head with his arms.

CHAPTER TWENTY TWO

"Where are we going?" Podner asked, digging his claws hard into Polly's hair.

"To get Sprog," she replied.

"What's Sprog,?"

"My little brother." Polly slowed to a jog. Podner gave a disbelieving grunt. "I've only just found him," she said.

"And now you've lost 'im."

Polly stood still. "No, I haven't. He's been kidnapped. Lady Serena's got him, somewhere near the old firework factory."

"If that's the way you want to go, then you'd better go right 'ere." Podner waved a paw in the direction of Courtleigh's back.

Polly put her fingers to her lips and whistled. Courtleigh skidded to a halt. "We're going the wrong way," she said.

"The old fireworks is this way. I remember it from back when," Podner said.

He scrambled up to the top of Polly's rucksack and pointed a paw in the direction he wanted them to go, the other he twisted round a strand of her hair.

It did not take long before the ground began to slope upwards and the tunnel looked more and more like a corridor, with brick walls and a wooden door at the end, under which Polly could see a thin line of daylight.

"Better wait 'ere. Rescuing's better in the dark." Podner slid off her shoulders and settling himself on the floor stretched his fat, little legs out in front of him. Polly shrugged off her rucksack and was about to join him, when her stomach growled.

"I'm starving," she sighed.

"So am I." Courtleigh took a deep breath. Sniffed, then sniffed again. A delicious smell of frying wafted in under the door. "Fish and chips," he said longingly. Polly's mouth watered. "Have you got any money?" he asked. She shook her head. Her insides echoed with emptiness. She wrapped her arms around herself and tried to think of something else, but the scent of crisp battered fish and crunchy fries grew stronger and stronger.

"I'm not staying here." Courtleigh could bear it no longer.

"Don't do it." Podner scrambled to his feet, but it was too late.

Daylight flooded into the tunnel as Courtleigh pushed open the door to a small storeroom. Vats of vinegar and boxes of salt stood on the shelves and they could smell the fat bubbling in the fryers downstairs.

"We're in the fish and chip shop," Courtleigh groaned. He strode over to the window and looked down into the yard. "I'm getting out of here."

"Oh no you're not." Podner scuttled over to the door. "You two get back in the cupboard and wait. I won't be long."

Courtleigh scowled. Polly shook her head. Podner waved his paws, bared his teeth and rushed at their ankles, like a terrier herding sheep. Hastily, they backed through the door.

"Stay there and don't move," Podner ordered.

"Where are you going?" Polly cried.

"You wait and see. Remember, I'm the best."

The door slammed and they blinked against the sudden darkness. Courtleigh slid slowly to the floor. Polly slumped down beside him. She sat with her head on her knees, miserably listening to their stomachs rumbling, for what seemed a long, long time, until at last there was a patter of paws, a scrumple of paper followed by the thick, hot smell of food.

"'Ere we are then. There's salt and vinegar on both."

"How did you do that?" Polly asked.

"Told you I'm the best. Never let anyone down. That's me, that's Podner."

They ate until the last scrap had gone, then Polly licked her fingers and Podner licked his paper and gave a contented sigh.

It grew dark. Courtleigh's eyes closed and he dreamed of rows of steel bright cages, each one holding a tiny Sprog, who rattled the bars and cried big, hot splashy tears.

"I can't find the key," he said, in his dream.

"We don't need a key," Podner's voice hissed in his ear. "Not to get out of 'ere we don't."

Courtleigh stretched. His back and legs were sore.

"We've got to go," Polly said urgently.

"O.K. Stay cool." Courtleigh slid himself up the wall. Polly moved over to the door and Podner scuttled after her.

"We're going down the back stairs, so don't make any noise," he whispered.

They crept down the wooden staircase and into a small back hall. Through a crack in the door, they could see the greenish, white light of the fish and chip shop. A long queue stood at the counter and behind it, two girls with plastic caps on their head were rushing about scooping freshly fried food on to greaseproof paper, wrapping it tightly against the cold and ringing up the money on the till. Courtleigh put out his hand to shut the door, but Podner shook his head.

"They always keep it open. Wait 'til no one's looking, then make a dash for the outside."

"They'll see us," Polly objected.

"We're not going through the shop. We're going out the back way." Podner jerked his head towards another door. "It goes into the yard.

Then down the alley and out into the street."

"Marie, I'm out of ketchup. I'm going out the back to get some." The door from the shop began to open.

"Now," Podner hissed. He jumped up to reach the handle, but Polly was there before him. She pushed open the door and they slipped out into the dark.

The girl, who had gone to get the ketchup, shivered. She crossed her fingers as she went up the stairs. She had always thought there was something strange about this place. People had been seen coming and going, in places where they should not have been and things disappeared. Only this evening, she had put three portions of cod and chips down on the counter only to find them gone and the customer empty handed. Marie hadn't believed her, joked that she was losing her mind, but she wasn't, she knew what she had done. It was the shop. It gave her the creeps. Grabbing a bottle of vinegar, she fled back into the light.

Out in the street, Podner insisted on jumping on top of Polly's rucksack.

"I see better up 'ere," he said, twisting his paw through her hair.

"OK. But don't pull," she told him.

"I won't. Except when I tell you which way to go," he agreed.

"You don't need to. Courtleigh knows where we're going."

"Humph," Podner gave a sulky grunt, then clung on tight as they set off down the street.

There was a row of red brick terraces, a couple of street lamps and then the road ended suddenly, as if someone had chopped it in two and thrown away the other piece. In front of them was a smooth, green lawn and in the middle of it a gleaming white building, shaped like a shoe box with three bands of black windows running round it and a door at the front. It was surrounded by a wall and the only way in appeared to be through a spiked black gate with sentry posts on either side. Lights beamed down into the courtyard beyond and they could see the shadows of dogs with sharp pointed ears.

"How are we going to get in there?" Polly said.

"Not that way." Courtleigh glanced at the guards. Dressed in black, they stood staring into the night.

"They've got guns," Polly whispered in horror. Her hand clutched her lucky charm. Podner's paws tightened in her hair.

"We'll have to go round the back," Courtleigh said.

"But they'll see us."

"So," Courtleigh shrugged. "They can't stop us. The road's not private or anything."

"Football," Podner said suddenly.

He's gone mad. Polly and Courtleigh looked at each other, as the same thought flashed across their mind.

"On the grass. You could be playing football," Podner spoke slowly, as if he were trying to explain something very simple to a pair of idiots.

"And the guards won't think there's anything strange going on." Polly realized what he wanted them to do. "It's a great idea Podner, except we haven't got a ball."

Even as she spoke, something fluttered and ruffled in her rucksack. Podner shifted himself on her shoulders, the flap rose a little and Blanket slid out. For a moment, it hovered in the air, then curled itself up into a tight white ball and settled firmly on the ground.

"We can't kick it," Polly cried.

"No, man, but we can throw it, then we won't hurt it." Courtleigh picked up Blanket. Holding it up high, he ran into the middle of the green. "Catch," he cried and Blanket sailed into the air and landed in Polly's outstretched hand.

Running, catching and calling, they dodged their way round the outside walls. There was no break in the smooth white expanse, until they got to the back, where they found another pair of gates. These were locked and bolted and secured with heavy chains, but there were no guards. In case they were being watched by security cameras, Courtleigh threw Blanket as close to the gate as he dared, then he and Polly dived after him.

"Gedit," Podner screeched. "Goal!" he yelled as Polly's hands closed round Blanket.

"Shh," they hissed.

Podner clapped his paws over his mouth and they stared through the gates. In front of them was the main block of the factory, at the side a row of single story outbuildings, where the dogs were kenneled. As they moved closer, there was a rumbling growl and the pack padded round the corner. Their eyes glinted in the brilliance of the security lights and when they snarled, their teeth were sharp and keen.

"Now what do we do? There's no way in," Polly said miserably.

"I'll think of something. In a minute," Courtleigh said.

Polly thought of Sprog, scared and lonely, locked up in somewhere in that building and clenched her fists.

"There's over the wall," Podner said.

"Yeah man, great if you can fly, but me, I've got no wings," Courtleigh said dismissively. Unnoticed, Blanket began to uncurl.

"And there's the dogs," Polly reminded them.

"They don't look that bad to me," Courtleigh said.

Polly took another glance. "They're worse than Brutus," she said.

"Nah," Courtleigh shook his head.

"I could distract them," said Podner. "I could turn myself into a furry ball. Like this." He ran to the gate and slid through the bars.

"Podner, no," Courtleigh yelled, as the dogs threw themselves at the small yellow creature.

Courtleigh charged the gates. As his hands closed round the bars, he remembered Brutus the unhappy dog, that no one loved. He had felt his pain and now as he stared desperately at the dogs that were tearing

167

Podner to pieces, he was filled with their fierce misery. These animals were not vicious, they were lost. They had a terrible need for a leader, for someone to tell them what to do.

Inside his head, something woke. There was a redness, then a band of steel white light. He opened his mouth and growled softly. The dogs lifted their heads, their ears pricked and they began to back away, leaving behind them a mangled piece of fur.

Blanket ballooned out of Polly's hands. She grabbed at the corners and as she held on tight, it began to rise up into the air. Slowly, very slowly, her feet left the ground. On the other side of the wall, Podner groaned faintly. Blanket shook itself, the air billowed up inside it and Polly shot upwards. The dogs slunk down on their haunches watching. Polly bit her lip. Blanket trembled, but Courtleigh growled a command and the dogs did not move, as the improvised balloon floated to the ground.

Podner lay on his back. His fur was torn, his ear bleeding. As Blanket deflated and settled on her shoulders, Polly picked him up and he buried his face in her jumper.

The dogs froze, their eyes fixed on Courtleigh. He stood very still, not daring to move in case he broke the link between them. His mind locked into theirs. He was their leader, they would do what he said. This was his magic. This was his power. At long last he had come into his own.

CHAPTER TWENTY THREE

Polly ran towards the Bioflex building looking for a way in, but there was no door. Nothing but a smooth white wall. The only entrance was at the front. As she crept round the corner, a long dark car drew up. Dr Lindstrom got out, followed by Lady Serena. Staring straight past him, she strode up the steps, her long white coat flowing behind her.

As the doctor turned to lock the car, Podner twisted out of Polly's arms and scuttled up the steps and dived under the skirt of Lady Serena's coat.

"We've work to do," she said as Dr Lindstrom joined her. The door slid open and with Podner at her heels she stepped inside.

The reception area sparkled with crystal and marble, a chandelier hung from the ceiling and the walls were covered with mirrored glass. There was nowhere to hide. Podner's only hope was the desk at the far end of the room, which threw a shadow on the highly polished floor. As Lady Serena turned to speak to the doctor, he took a deep breath, curled himself into a ball and rolled as fast and as far as he could. He came to a stop with his nose pressed against the leg of the desk. No one had seen him, now he had to find a way of getting Polly inside.

"Check the doors and reset the alarms. Tell Security no one, but no one, is to be allowed inside the building tonight," Lady Serena ordered.

Dr Lindstrom walked over to the desk and keyed in a series of numbers. Crouched under the desk, Podner counted on his claws.

"Two to the right, three to the left," he muttered. "Two to the right, three to the left," he repeated.

"It's all secure," the doctor said.

"Good. I'm going to start on the boy."

"Tonight?" Dr Lindstrom asked.

"As soon as we've opened up the lab, but first there are one or two things in the office to be sorted out," Lady Serena said.

Podner heard their footsteps moving away. He opened one eye and saw the end of Lady Serena's coat disappearing down the corridor. When he was sure they were gone, he came out of his hiding place.

"Two to the right, three to the left," he muttered. If that was the way to lock the doors, then to open them, he would have to press the keys in the reverse order.

The desk was made of white marble and the legs on either side were two round pillars. He flexed his claws, made a little run and jumped. He landed half way up a pillar. For a moment, he managed to cling to the smooth surface, then with a horrible scraping sound, he slid slowly to the ground.

He picked himself up and took another run at the desk. His arms waved frantically as he grabbed at the top, missed and crashed onto the marble floor. As he fell, his foot snagged a leather waste bin and tipped it over onto its side. Podner picked himself up gave himself a shake, then upending the bin, pushed it as close to the desk as he could and scrambled on top of it. Standing on his toes and stretching out his arms, he could almost reach the top. He breathed in and jumped. The air in his lungs acted like a balloon giving him extra lift. This time he landed on his stomach, hurtling towards the key pad.

"Three to the right. Two to the left," he muttered as he tapped in the numbers. The doors slid open, there was a pause, then Polly stepped into reception.

"How did you do that?" she said.

"I told you I am the best," Podner preened.

"Where's Sprog then."

"I don't know exactly, but when I was under that desk thing I 'eard that woman say they 'ad to experiment on the boy tonight. I think she wants to see what's inside his 'ead."

Polly thought of the cold, green eyes in that smooth white face and shivered. "We've got to find him," she said.

"That's easy. They're taking 'im to the labs."

"Yeah, but they could be anywhere. This place is huge. What's that?" She pointed to the key pad.

"It opens doors and things."

"What sort of things?" Polly said.

"Security and stuff."

Alarms and cameras, Polly thought. *And maybe a map to show where they were, so the guards could check on them.* She stared so hard at the numbers that her eyes began to blur.

"'Urry up. They'll be back soon," Podner pulled at her sleeve. Polly brushed him away. Her lucky charm bumped against her chest and she clutched it, because sometimes it helped her think. 1547. The moment she touched the twisted piece of wood, the figures flashed across her brain. She leaned over and punched in the numbers. A map of the building came up on the surface.

"That's where we've got to go." Polly pointed at the square, which said Laboratory.

Podner jumped up onto her shoulders and held on tight as she made her way through the maze of corridors. Each one looked the same, white walls, white floors, white doors, but with the map in her head Polly did not hesitate.

"This is it," she said, when they had walked for about five minutes.

"We can't go in," Podner objected. "They might be in there."

Polly knew he was right, but she did not know what to do next.

"There's got to be a way," she said.

Like a grey ghost, Blanket slid out of the rucksack. It sailed down and spread itself on the floor, getting thinner and thinner, until it vanished through the crack under the door. They waited. It was so quiet, Polly could hear herself breathe. Podner twisted his claws in her hair. She hardly noticed, all she cared about was finding Sprog. At last Blanket reappeared. It billowed up and waved its edge at them.

"Go on then," Podner whispered. "Blanket says it's all right."

The first room they came to had no windows and was full of computers. At the far end there was another door. When Blanket had checked to see if it was safe, they followed it into a wide corridor, where the light was dim and the walls were lined with cages. Each one had a bed and a table, on which stood a metal drinking bowl. Hanging from the bars was a short chain with a bright steel collar. A camera was focused on each cage, to record the actions of whatever creature was inside.

"That's not right," Podner hissed. Polly nodded; her stomach was tight and she felt sick.

They hurried past the cages and into another corridor. Blanket began to get very excited. It billowed into full sail and sped forward, until flapping its edges, it swirled to a stop and waved frantically at them.

"He's in there," Polly whispered.

Podner pressed his ear to the door. "Quick, there's someone coming," he cried.

He grabbed at Polly's leg; she threw herself at the nearest door and as Dr Linsdstrom stepped out of the lab, they fell into total blackness.

"This is not doing my 'ead any good," Podner groaned, as he tried to lift Polly's elbow from his face.

"Stop it. You're pinching me," Polly hissed through a mouthful of grubby wool.

Blanket gave a little shake and rose into the air. Polly sat up and Podner ran his paws over his face to check for broken bones.

"Where are we?" Polly stood up to look and instantly ducked down again.

"There's a window and you can look right into the next room," she whispered.

"Let's see." Podner stretched himself up to his full height.

"No. Don't. They'll see us." Polly grasped a handful of fur and pulled him down beside her.

Blanket floated away and hovered in front of the window. Polly groaned and braced herself for the moment when Lady Serena or the doctor burst in and dragged them out of their hiding place, but nothing happened.

"I don't think they can see us," Podner said, after a while.

"That window must be one of those one way mirrors. We can see out, but they can't see in and that's why it's so dark in here," Polly said.

The room, on the other side of the glass, was brightly lit. On one side there was a bank of machines, straight in front of them was a computer, with a very large screen. In the middle was the sort of chair that you find in a dentist's surgery. Beside it was a steel trolley, where Lady Serena stood with her back to them setting out some sharp instruments on a glass tray.

"Put him in the chair," she said, as Dr Lindstrom came in leading Sprog by the hand.

"Now David, we want to see what you can do," she said, as the doctor strapped him down. "Do you understand?" Sprog looked up at her with big brown eyes. "Do you?" she repeated.

Sprog stared at the screen. Nothing happened. Lady Serena tapped her long red finger nails against the smooth steel trolley. "Come on David, be a good boy," she said, her voice low with menace. Sprog's shoulders drooped a little; he tried to lift his hand to put his thumb in his mouth, but the straps held him down. "We know you can make things happen. We just want to find out how."

Sprog's eyes were fixed on the screen. It was blank. Dr Lindstrom shook his head.

"He can do it. He will do it," Lady Serena insisted. She picked up a steel cap. "Since he won't co-operate, we'll jump start the process." Dr Lindstrom took the cap and set it carefully on Sprog's head. "This won't hurt a bit," Lady Serena said softly.

The doctor stepped back out of sight and pressed a switch. Sprog screwed up his eyes and Blanket flung itself at the glass, beating wildly in a desperate attempt to break through. The computer screen fuzzed.

White spots danced frantically, then came together in a Blanket like shape.

"See," Lady Serena said. "I was right. Increase the power."

"No!" Polly screamed.

The screen crackled, went blank, then a picture appeared. It showed a smallish, squarish girl with brown hair, her fists clenched, mouth wide open and beside her a furry creature, leaping up and down in rage.

"Brilliant," Lady Serena sighed. She lifted the cap and gently stroked Sprog's hair.

"My good, little boy," she murmured.

"Leave him alone," Polly banged her fists against the glass. Podner growled fiercely. They were both so intent on what was going on in the lab that neither of them heard the door to the viewing room open.

"Got you." Dr Lindstrom's hand came down hard on Polly's neck. She kicked and scratched, but he lifted her up like a puppy. "Look what we have here," he said, throwing her at Lady Serena's feet.

"It's the girl on the screen. How fascinating. She looks quite ordinary, but she must be linked in some way to the boy." Lady Serene turned cold green eyes on Polly. "Interesting. He seems to react to her more than anything else. I think we can use her."

"And there's this." Dr Lindstrom held up Podner. "This is not so ordinary."

"No, it's not." Lady Serena frowned and ran a long sharp nail down

Podner's front. "I've seen one of these before, but I can't remember where or when. Whatever it is, we'll examine it with the girl. It may be important. In fact I rather think it is. For the time being put them in cages."

Polly scrambled to her feet and made a dash for the door, but before she could reach it, Dr Lindstrom had her by the arm. "You can't keep us here. We'll be missed. Miss A will tell the Police," Polly yelled.

"You're from St. Savlon's. No one will miss you," Lady Serena said coldly. Sprog made a faint choking sound and closed his eyes. "Take them away. We've got work to do," Lady Serena said.

Sprog screwed up his eyes to keep the tears from falling down his cheeks. It was his fault that Polly had been caught. He hadn't meant to put her picture on the screen, but he had been so pleased to see her. He hated it here. The dark lady frightened him. She kept trying to make him do things, but even if they put that thing on his head that hurt so much, he would not do what they said.

"He's getting tired," Lady Serena said when the doctor returned.

"He's being stubborn," the doctor replied.

"It doesn't matter. What matters is that I was right. This child is the link we've been looking for. With him I can prove that what we call magic and what we call science are one and the same. He has this ability to affect computers, which is something we can measure, and if we can measure it, we can understand it and if we can understand it we can control it and if we can control it," Lady Serena snapped her fingers, "it will become just another form of technology."

"And if we own the technology, it will make us very rich and very powerful," Dr Lindstrom said.

"Money," Lady Serena tossed her head, "what does that matter? What matters is that there will be no more magic." Her long, white fingers rested on Sprog's shoulders. "Time for bed, my little boy," she said softly.

"Shall I put him back in his cage?"

"No. I don't want him near the others. His brain needs a rest. Take him to the Dark Chamber and we will work on him again later."

As the doctor carried Sprog away, Blanket slid under the door of the viewing room. and followed.

CHAPTER TWENTY FOUR

Courtleigh was getting tired. The dog part of his brain was taking over and he couldn't stop it. His eyes closed, his legs wobbled and he sank to the ground. Behind the fence the puzzled dogs lay and waited as their leader slept. .

It was almost morning, when he lifted his head to the wind and sniffed. There were no strange scents on the air, no intruders. He raised his front leg to scratch for fleas behind his ear and then he remembered and a cold, sick feeling flipped over in his stomach. He was not the leader of a pack of dogs, he was Courtleigh Jones and somewhere in that sleek, white building in front of him, were Polly, Podner and Sprog.

He got up and peered through the gate. As soon as he moved, the guard dogs came running, their tails wagging, their tongues hanging out. He slipped his hand through the bars and patted them. Soon they would be shut in the kennels and his last hope of getting inside would be gone. The wall was too smooth to climb and too high to jump.

Courtleigh walked round the building, making sure that the dogs were with him. The guards at the front gate looked tired and bored.

He stood and watched them for a while, then picked up a stone and threw it as hard as he could into the middle of the pack. The dogs yelped in surprise. The guards swung round to see what had caused the commotion and Courtleigh slipped in behind them and ran, as fast as he could, towards the kennels, where he could hide, until he found a way of getting inside.

The dogs bounded along beside him as he made for an open door. Their growls were friendly and playful; they butted against his legs and pretended to snap at his heels, and he yapped and growled with them, until a shrill screech in his brain screamed, "Stop!" He slid to a halt and stood panting, while around him the other dogs sat, their eyes fixed on the man with the whistle. The handler walked slowly round Courtleigh, shaking his head in puzzlement.

"Are you boy or dog? You look like a boy, but the dogs think you're one of them. I've never seen anything like it. Never. If anyone they don't know gets in here, they're trained to tear them apart, but you haven't got a scratch on you."

A bark rose in Courtleigh's throat and he swallowed it down. He knew there were words he must say somewhere in his brain, but it was too late.

"Grab him," the security guard shouted.

The dogs growled, softly. "Easy boys," the handler soothed.

"Intruder," the guard panted. "Got to get him inside." The dogs' growling deepened and the guard stepped back quickly. "What's going on?" he demanded.

"Bust if I know. He doesn't look very dangerous to me," the handler replied.

"Whether he is, or he isn't, he's coming with me and you can keep those brutes of yours out of the way," the guard said.

The handler scratched his head. For a moment Courtleigh thought that he was going to refuse, then he gestured sharply and the dogs backed away. The guard took hold of his arm and twisted it hard behind his back.

"Where are you taking me? You can't do this. I want my social worker. I'm in care," he yelled.

"You're from St. Savlons and we all know what sort go there." The guard sneered, tightening his grip. "Don't you worry. Lady S will know what to do with you. She runs a programme for kids like you. Works wonders with them, apparently." He laughed, nastily and gave Courtleigh's arm another twist. "Especially good with the wild ones, she is. Those that go barging in where they shouldn't."

Podner lay on the floor of his cage and put his paws over his head. Fat lot of good they were as rescuers, locked up with chains round their necks waiting for Lady Serena and that doctor with the cold eyes to open up their heads and look inside their brains.

"Podner," Polly whispered, "are you all right?"

"No," he growled and curled up into a tight ball of despair.

Polly scowled. Now, when she needed all the help she could get to stop herself from panicking, Podner wasn't even speaking to her, let alone helping her to find a way out of this cage. "Don't talk to me then," she snarled. There was no response. "See if I care," she added. Furiously, she stared up at the camera. "You can't keep us here. You can't," she yelled, banging at the bars.

Podner groaned. *I'll think of something* Polly thought. *And Courtleigh will too. He's probably gone to find Miss A right now. She won't let anything happen to us. I know she won't. We'll be all right.* Her fingers closed round her lucky charm and she felt a little bit better.

The door opened and Dr Lindstrom came in leading Courtleigh. His hands were tied behind his back and there was a chain around his neck. "We will decide what we're going to do with you later. You could be an interesting control for our experiments," the doctor said, as he locked him into a cage.

"No way man," Courtleigh glared defiantly at the doctor. "You're not doing no experiments on me." The doctor looked at him with his pale, blue eyes and Courtleigh felt something cold and heavy turn over inside him.

"Courtleigh," Polly whispered, when the doctor had gone, "what are we going to do?"

CHAPTER TWENTY FIVE

The Slurge did not like waking up. Curled nose to toe in his warm cubby hole, he'd been asleep for weeks, when the ringing noise started. At first he tried to ignore it, but it grew louder and louder, screeching through his head, until he had to stop it. Opening one eye, he peered through a curtain of hair. Somewhere in his nest of old rags was the switch. He slapped his huge hands around, until he hit it and the sound stopped. It was time to get up. They needed him in the labs and he had to be there, or they would send him away, like the others that had got stuck in their changes.

The Slurge opened his mouth to yawn and a roar shook the storage cupboard, where he slept. He stretched and scratched and smoothed down the ragged mat of hair that completely covered his body. Then he pulled on a pair of dark brown cords and an old lab coat and slurped down the corridor, the pads of his feet making sucking sounds on the smooth white floors.

There were three new ones in the cages. A brown skinned one with short dark curly fur all over its head, a smaller, fatter one with a white face and a flat, furry thing lying on the floor making puddles from its eyes. After looking them all over, he decided he would start with the middle one.

Polly looked up at the huge creature bearing down on her. Its head reached almost to the ceiling, its long arms hung down to its knees. It wore a brown overall and trousers tied round its waist with string, but its large, flat feet were bare. Taking a key out of its pocket, it muttered and growled, as it unlocked the door of the cage.

"I won't be scared," she told herself, staring defiantly at the creature. Her gaze met his and under the fall of hair his eyes were brown and sad. Then he reached in and pulled her roughly out of the cage. With her chain wrapped tightly round his massive wrist, he brought out Courtleigh, then Podner and led them, like dogs on a leash, to the bathroom. Locked inside the cubicle, Polly looked round for a way to escape, but there were no windows, the walls were stainless steel and the creature was guarding the only door.

Back in their cages, they were fed. The creature opened a small flap and slammed down bowls of lumpy, grey gloop. It looked like wall paper paste, but smelled like porridge. Polly's stomach rumbled. There was no spoon, so she dipped her finger in the mess.

"There's no sugar," she spluttered.

"It's better than nothing," Courtleigh said.

Polly made a face. "It's disgusting. I don't know how you can even

184

think of eating it," she said, raising her eyes to the roof. The black eye of the camera stared back at her. Polly grinned. Perhaps the porridge wasn't that bad after all. Taking a large handful, she stretched up as far as she could and plastered it all over the lens. "That's fixed it," she said.

"Too cool, man." Courtleigh splodged gloop all over his camera.

"Now you Podner."

Podner stared up at the roof of his cage and said with great dignity. "Ow am I supposed to get up there?"

"Jump man. You can do it."

"And let this 'ere chain round my neck choke me to death?" Polly and Courtleigh's faces fell, but Podner continued, "I've got a much better idea." He snuffled up a mouthful of goo, chewed for a minute or two, then spat. "'Ow about that then?" he said proudly. He looked up at the three cameras. All were completely covered.

"Now we've got to get out of here," Polly said. She wished she still had her rucksack. In it was her penknife and a long, thin piece of wire, but the rucksack with all her precious things was on the floor of the viewing room. "Where's Sprog? Why haven't they brought him here?"

"They might still be looking at his brain," Courtleigh said, with a shudder.

"With that hat thing. It's not fair. He's only little. He's never done anything to anybody." Polly grabbed at the bars and rattled them hard. "He's my brother and they can't do this to him." She kicked at the sides of the cage, stamped her feet on the floor and banged her head against the bars. "He's the only family thing I've got left, except this." She stuck her hand down her jumper and pulled out her lucky charm. "And it's not doing any good." She tugged at the string, trying to pull it from her neck.

"Stop!" Podner shouted, bouncing up and down in his cage, his fur standing on end with excitement. "You've got it," he yelled. "You've got the key."

"What?" Polly looked at the dried up piece of twig she held in her hand.

Podner took a deep breath. "It's a dragon's claw," he said reverently.

"I thought you said it was a key."

"It is. It's the key to everything. Well, most things."

Polly's fingers began to tingle, the palms of her hands grew hot and a surge of energy shot up her arms. "If it's a key, then it will open things," she said in wonder.

"Like cages man. So come on."

Polly lifted the claw to her neck. The collar came loose and clattered to the ground. Next she slid it into the padlock and stepped out of the cage, then she freed Courtleigh and Podner.

"Look out for that huge furry thing. I don't like the look of that; I don't like the look of that at all," Podner fussed, as they stepped cautiously into the corridor.

"It'll be OK. All we've got to do is get Sprog," Polly said.

"But where is 'e?" Podner rubbed his eyes against the hard, white light. "'E might be in the lab still and I'm not going back in there."

Polly thought of what Lady Serena and the doctor might be doing to her little brother and she clenched her fists.

"Stay cool man, we'll find him." Courtleigh looked down the long, white corridor and crossed his fingers, behind his back. All the corridors looked the same. They could go up and down them for ever and never find the right one. Polly screwed up her eyes and tried to remember the map in her head.

"It's this way," she said.

"We've been 'ere before," Podner said, after a while.

"We haven't," Polly snapped, although she was not sure.

"We have," Courtleigh said.

Polly felt herself getting cross. Her head was getting hotter and the breath was spiraling down out of her nose. Podner froze, his mouth dropped open in surprise and pointing at Polly he shouted,

"Stop it."

"Shut it." Courtleigh scooped him up and slapped his hand over his mouth. Podner's legs kicked in the air, his eyes bulged, his paws waved wildly as he tried to get their attention. He struggled and choked, until finally Polly and Courtleigh saw Blanket, floating like a ghost a few feet from the ground, almost invisible against the white walls. It beckoned

187

and they followed, along corridors, down staircases, through empty rooms, until at last, they came to the door of the Dark Chamber, where Blanket crumpled and laid its edge on Polly's shoulder, as if to say it didn't know what to do next.

She pointed the claw and the door opened. From somewhere far below them came a faint hiss. It was dark on the stairs. Blanket went first, then Polly, feeling her way carefully to stop herself missing a step. Podner followed, bumping down on his bottom, as his legs were too short to manage the steps. Courtleigh went last.

They were half way down when the door swung shut, leaving them in a dim half light. The hissing grew louder. Polly felt for the next step. She leaned forward, then almost fell as Blanket twisted in panic around her face. She tried to push it away, but it clung on, quivering with terror at the sound of something slapping its way through water.

"Don't move," Courtleigh whispered.

It was happening again, part of him was becoming whatever was out there in the darkness. He felt the cold slide through his veins. His arms and legs grew heavy. The air burned his lungs. He wanted to be there with the others, slipping through the cool dark, ducking down beneath the surface to let the oxygen slide through his gills.

"Where are you going? What do you want?" their voices hissed through his head.

"We want to get past," Courtleigh said out loud.

"No one gets past us. We guard the Dark Chamber."

"You have to let us through."

"What have you brought us? Have you brought us an arm or a leg. It's almost feeding time and we are hungry."

Courtleigh's stomach clenched. He licked his lips and tasted raw fish. A long, white tentacle snaked out of the water and began to feel its way up the steps.

"If you haven't got anything, we'll have to make do with you."

"You can't eat me," Courtleigh said. "Because I know what you are."

"Oh no you don't. No one does. No one cares," the voices wept.

Courtleigh edged his way past Polly and Podner. When he reached the bottom step, something curled round his ankle. He ignored it and squatted down by the side of the pool. "You used to live on land and you could change your shapes when you felt like it. You could be...," he stopped and let the creatures slide into his mind. "Alligators and crocodiles and octopuses and anacondas and ..." He paused and gave Blanket a tug towards the plank of wood that spanned the water. "And DRAGONS," he lied.

There was a long, loud sigh and as the creatures thought sadly of what they had once been, Polly, Blanket and Podner hurried across the bridge.

"Dragons are the best," something hissed.

"No they're not," something else growled.

Yes they are."

There was a snap and a roar and a lash of a tail. Courtleigh jumped to his feet and ran after the others, as the creatures leaped upon each other and bloodstained water surged over the edge of the pool.

CHAPTER TWENTY SIX

In the Dark Chamber, Sprog curled his knees up to his chest and covered his head with his arms. He was tired and scared. His ears ached from listening to the silence and his eyes hurt from staring through the dark. He rubbed them and a speck of red light appeared on the wall. He blinked and the light grew longer, stretching itself out into a long, thin line in the shape of a door.

Then Blanket was wrapping itself around him and Polly's hand slipped into his and she was pulling him off the bed, just as Courtleigh burst in and said they'd got to get out quick before the monsters stopped fighting. His legs shook so much that he couldn't run, so Courtleigh picked him up and he held on tight as they hurried over the bridge.

Beneath them, the creatures snarled and snapped. The water roiled and boiled. It surged over their feet and then slopped back into the pool. Everything went very, very still. A half fish, half alligator floated to the surface. The fight was over and the creatures were hungry.

Courtleigh's legs ached and it was hard to breathe with Sprog clinging to his neck. Podner panted hard as he used his arms to pull himself up the steps. Polly glanced behind her, something long and scaly was crawling up the stairs and the door at the top was still shut. She pointed the claw and willed it to open. Nothing happened and with a triumphant hiss, a tentacle twisted round her ankle.

Polly kicked out as hard as she could, but the creature's grip tightened, knocking her off balance. She was tipping over, she was falling...

Podner leapt. His teeth sank into hard rubbery flesh. There was a terrible hiss and oily black **blood** spurted into his mouth. Furiously, he stuck his claws into the **creature**. Polly shrieked and tumbled forwards, knocking Courtleigh **and Sprog** sideways, as the wounded monster slithered downwards and **the door** swung open. Podner clung onto the edge of a step. He coughed **and** spat, then pulling himself up, he thrust his paw into the air and climbed after the others.

Slamming the door on the monsters, Polly peered down the corridor. It was empty, but in the bright white light there was nowhere to hide. Anyone coming round the corner could see them. They had to find the way out and soon, before the big, hairy thing realized they were missing. The trouble was, she had no idea where they were. She screwed up her eyes and tried to think.

Sloop, sloop, sloop. The Slurge's feet made sucking noises on the floor. His arms swung, his head swayed from side to side and, as the scent of human children grew stronger, he growled softly from the back of his throat.

"I can hear something," Polly said.

At the far end of the corridor, Courtleigh pushed against the nearest door.

"In here. Quick."

Polly pointed the claw, but it was too late. The Slurge was lumbering towards them, his eyes glowing red with fury, his snarl rising into a roar, while from the other direction came Lady Serena and the Doctor.

"Put the boy down and give me the dragon's claw." Lady Serena's voice was cold as an Arctic wind.

"Won't." Polly balled her hands into fists. Sprog buried his face in Courtleigh's back and Podner tried very, very hard to be brave and not hide behind his legs.

"I think you will." Lady Serena waved her hand and the Slurge loomed above them, baring yellow teeth and purple tongue. "Tearit, tearit," came from the back of his throat, as he leaned closer and closer.

"No you won't. I don't want them damaged. But I do want that claw. So stay and guard, but don't touch. Dr Lindstrom will keep an eye on you all, until I get back with the injections."

The Slurge made grinding noises with his teeth. Sprog gave a frightened, little snuffle and Podner shut his eyes. Courtleigh stepped back against the wall. Polly's stomach turned a somersault, but she did not drop her glance. Lady Serena was the scariest thing she had ever seen, far worse than the drooling, snarling Slurge or the cold eyed doctor, but she was not going to show her fear.

Lady Serena gave them one final look, turned to go, then stopped as a phone rang. She picked up one of the receivers set into the wall.

"Security here, Mam. There's a bit of a problem at the gate."

"Deal with it."

"It's the Police, Mam. They say they have to speak to you."

Lady Serena tapped her long, red nails against the wall. "Not now. I'm busy."

There was a pause, then the sound of muffled voices. Finally the guard said, "I'm sorry, Mam, but they say it can't wait. It's about some children, who've gone missing from St. Savlons."

They were saved. Lady Serena would have to take them to the gate, where Miss Abramawitch would be waiting. She would be very, very cross, but when they explained she would understand. Polly glanced at Courtleigh and bit her cheek to stop herself from grinning. Courtleigh shifted Sprog's weight and promised himself that he would never, ever again take anything that didn't really belong to him.

Lady Serena laughed. "St. Savlons," she said, "is that all? Tell them I'm in the middle of a vital piece of research and I'll be down as soon as I can. They won't mind. After all, when did anyone care about children from St. Savlons? They are simply not that important."

Not important! How could she say that! Polly's brain whirled. She saw Shaz, Baz and Maz scrying to help her find Sprog. Courtleigh saving her from the fire at the Harris'. Sprog tied down in that terrible chair. They were all trouble, but he had done nothing wrong. And now Lady Serena and the doctor were going to hurt him even more and they thought no one cared, but she did, she cared very, very much indeed.

The sudden spurt of flame sent them flying. Courtleigh fell back against one wall, the doctor against the other. The Slurge gave a terrified howl and fled. Podner jumped up and down and shouted,

"More, Polly, more."

The fury flared up from her stomach; flames roared from her mouth and leapt from her fingers. Fire ran up the walls and danced on the ceiling.

"Brilliant!" Lady Serena gasped, as the edge of her coat ignited. "Hold her," she screamed at the doctor, who covered his head, as his hair began to sizzle. Smoke swirled through the corridor; the floor began to melt.

"Way to go!" Courtleigh cried.

Polly took a deep breath. The air rumbled, light and heat zigzagged from wall to wall and the whole building burst into flame.

CHAPTER TWENTY SEVEN

Courtleigh tore out of the blazing building. Sprog's arms tight around his throat, Blanket twisting round his waist and Podner clinging desperately to his hand, legs whirling in the air, as he was pulled along. Coughing and choking, he stumbled down the steps, straight into one of the firemen.

"It's all right. You're safe. Let me take the little lad."

Sprog's grip loosened and he let himself be lifted from Courtleigh's back. Holding tight onto Blanket, he was handed to a girl with blonde hair and blue eyes, who set him down on the ground and spoke to him softly. Podner scuttled over to them and disappeared into a large patchwork bag.

"Is there anyone else in the building?" a firemen shouted into a megaphone.

Courtleigh swiveled round. "Where's Polly?" he croaked.

Polly strolled among the flames, watching the way they ate up the walls, and curled along the ceilings. Her skin glowed, her hair crackled and she hummed to herself, as she danced over the burning floors. She had never felt so happy, or so strong. The blood was roaring in her veins and she could feel the power growing in her body. Then, just as she felt she could do anything she wanted in the whole world, a great wet whoosh of water almost knocked her off her feet. Six firemen carrying a thick black hose thundered in through the door.

"I've found her," one shouted. "I'm bringing her out."

"Let me go," Polly shrieked, as he threw her over his shoulder and carried her screaming and kicking into the fresh air.

There were four fire engines, two ambulances and half a dozen police cars in the courtyard. Lady Serena, her coat blackened and singed, stood talking to an Inspector.

"I can't imagine who could have started this fire, or why they should want to. The Bioflex Foundation was searching for a cure for this terrible, new black spot virus and now all our ground breaking work has been destroyed. This is a deliberate act and you must do your very best to catch these criminals."

"Oh we will, Mam. You may rely on it," the Inspector said.

"It's her," Courtleigh hissed. "She's the one who snatched Sprog and put us in cages."

"Go and get in the car. It's outside the gates," the girl with the blonde hair said quietly. "Sprog, Podner and Blanket are already there. I'll go and get Polly." Without waiting to see whether he would do as she said, she walked over to the firemen. "I think that's one of the missing children from St. Savlons. I work there, so if you'd like me to take her,

197

my car's outside."

"The sooner the better Miss. You'd have thought she wanted to stay in there, the way she's been carrying on."

The fireman bent his knees and set Polly on the ground. She clenched her fists and scowled.

"I was all right," she muttered. The girl gave her a look that made Polly think of Miss Abramawitch. She swallowed quickly and said, "But thank you for rescuing me."

They walked together to the red car. Courtleigh and Sprog were sitting in the back. Podner was lying on the front seat.

"I was keeping it warm for you," he said, sliding down and settling himself on the floor.

"Where are we going?" Polly asked, as she fastened her seat belt.

"To St. Savlons," the girl said and Courtleigh groaned.

"But we can't," Polly cried.

"There is nowhere else for you to go," the girl said.

Sprog gave a little whimper and holding Blanket against his cheek, snuggled up against Courtleigh.

In the Winter twilight, St. Savlons loomed like a fortress in front of them, its turrets black and forbidding against the orange sky. Polly thought of the empty echoing rooms, the Blatches with their disinfectants and their sprays and felt a cold misery settle in the pit of her stomach. Courtleigh bit his lip and stared out of the side window at the notice hanging on the gate.

St. Savlons don't care home, he thought, bitterly.

Home! Polly blinked furiously. St. Savlons was nothing like any home she'd ever imagined and she was going to be stuck here for the rest of her life.

Home is with Gran, thought Courtleigh. *Not in this place.*

They drove through the gates and pulled up at the front door. The car stopped, but no one moved. The blonde girl turned and looked at them. Her blue eyes were violet in the half light and she gave a little growl from the back of her throat.

"OK. I'm going," Polly muttered, through clenched teeth. She climbed out of the car and Podner scurried after her.

"'Ere what about me?" he whispered, worriedly.

"I don't know. The Blatches will probably take you to the vets." Podner gasped and Polly took his paw. "But I won't let them," she promised.

They walked reluctantly up the steps. The girl pulled the bell rope and as it tolled deep inside the building, Polly thought of the night they had first arrived and looked at Courtleigh, who gave her a sort of half grin. They waited, but no one came. At last the girl gave the door a push, it opened and she ushered them inside.

The entrance hall was as dismal as ever. The lights were dim, throwing their shadows against walls, as they trailed down the corridor to the common room, where Shaz sprawled on the sofa filing her nails, Maz sat in front of the fire reading a magazine, while Baz played with the remote for the TV.

"Sprog!" shrieked Shaz. Leaping to her feet, she scooped him up and hugged him.

"You got him!"

"You rescued him." Baz thumped Courtleigh on the back, so hard he nearly fell over.

Maz grabbed Polly's hands, then dropped them, as her fingers closed round Podner's paw. "What's this, a real live teddy bear? Hey it's cute." She leaned over to pick him up, then jumped back as Podner bared his teeth and growled.

"That's Podner. He's with us," Polly said.

"Hi, Podner." Maz raised her hand. "Good to see you." Podner stretched out a paw and they shook.

"Cool," said Baz. Podner grinned and gave a little bow.

"He saved me from these monster things," Polly said.

"Oh yeah," Shaz scoffed.

"He did," Courtleigh said.

"Tell us," said Baz.

They settled themselves on the sofas and Polly and Courtleigh told how, with the help of Podner and Blanket, they had rescued Sprog.

"And all the time we were in the hospital with this terrible virus,"

Maz giggled.

"We were on the news and everything. The Blatches were too. They were having a great time with all those doctors trying to figure out what we'd got," said Baz.

"They thought it might spread all over the world. Imagine that!" Shaz opened her eyes wide and laughed.

"Trouble was, the only way to catch it was to drink bat pooh steeped in snot," said Maz.

"I think you'd rather have this." The blonde girl set down a tray filled with pizzas and fizzy drinks.

"No vitamins?" Shaz said.

"No pills?" Maz shook her head in disbelief, as they helped themselves to the sort of food that had never been seen before at St. Savlons.

"Has Mrs Blatch had a brain transplant or something?" Baz said, licking tomato sauce from her fingers.

"I don't care. This is great," Courtleigh sighed with contentment and Sprog giggled and blew bubbles down his straw.

"You won't be eating like this every day." Miss Abramawitch stood in the doorway.

"In fact, you don't really deserve it at all, since not one of you has behaved very well."

"That's not fair," Polly exploded. "Scythe kidnapped Sprog, so we had to get him back. We tried to tell you, but you wouldn't listen." Miss

Abramawitch looked at her.

"Well you wouldn't," Polly muttered.

"I didn't know what Scythe was up to. Once I found out, if you, Polly, hadn't set fire to the Bioflex building, we would have got you out."

"How did you know where we'd gone?"

"Your Gran, Courtleigh saw you in her crystal and the cats knew what to do."

"What about Lady Serena and the doctor, what's happened to them?" demanded Courtleigh.

"Nothing I bet," Polly scowled.

"Do we have any evidence?" Miss Abramawitch said coolly.

"It's all burned," Courtleigh muttered.

"So who do you think is going to believe you?" They looked miserably at each other. "It's a good thing I do," Jenny said softly. "But as far as the rest of the world is concerned, what are you but a pack of disruptive children, who nobody wants? You should think yourselves lucky that you have St. Savlons."

"And the Blatches," Polly groaned.

"The Blatches have resigned. Mrs Blatch has had a breakdown and Mr Blatch is looking after her, or the other way around. What you need now is a firm hand. A warden who knows exactly what you get up to. How you get out on Saturday nights."

She looked at Shaz, Baz and Maz, then turned to Courtleigh and

Polly. "How you two get past guard dogs and set fire to buildings."

"Yeah well," Courtleigh muttered.

"I didn't," Polly began. Miss Abramawitch gave her one of her looks. "Yeah all right. It was me," she admitted. "But they deserved it," she added.

"You see what I mean. If you are going to stay here, and there is no question about it, this is where you are going to be for the foreseeable future, you need someone who can deal with your rudeness, your disobedience, and the fact that you don't quite belong in the outside world. In fact you need someone like me."

"Like you?" Shaz echoed.

"Yes. I'm the new warden of St. Savlons," Miss Abramawitch smiled. "From now on you are all going to be living here with me and of course with Lucy."

The girl with the blue eyes and blonde hair smiled. Then quickly and gracefully, she transformed herself back into a cat.

What, Polly wondered, *was going to happen next?*

ABOUT THE AUTHOR

Misha Herwin is a writer of plays and stories. Her plays have been performed in England and Jamaica, by schools, theatre in education and adult theatre companies. Some have been published by Carel Press.

Currently she is enjoying teaching in a junior high school, in Leek and writing what happens next to Polly and Courtleigh.

Printed in the United Kingdom
by Lightning Source UK Ltd.
130270UK00001B/274-282/A